THE
JOURNEYMAN

A STORY OF HOPE
AND
PERSONAL WILL

BY
RIP GERBER

The Journeyman © Copyright 2020 by Rip Gerber

WISE
MEDIA GROUP

For rights, media & contact visit RipGerber.com

ISBN: 978-1629671994

Interior Formatting by Brian Schwartz.

Rev 23-5.22

PROLOGUE

It begins with two brothers chained to a wall in a dark room. I do not know them, but I know their Father locked them in that basement, where they had been living as prisoners since birth. Behind them was a wood furnace, but they had never seen it, since their feet and hands and heads were in shackles. They could see only the wall, and the shadows that danced upon it. Every day the Father walked to and from the burning furnace, carrying objects such as books and food and animals and furniture. The two boys spent their years in the darkness, naming the shadows that danced on the walls, for there was nothing else to do.

Through good fortune one boy escaped. Unshackled, he turned and was blinded by the furnace light. Eventually his eyes adjusted, and he could see the objects in the basement, but did not believe they were real, since he was so accustomed to seeing only the black shadows. He made his way up the stairs and outside, where the light from the sun blinded him again, until he saw shadows, then shapes and colors, and then all the glory of the world was exposed to him, and he was overcome with joy.

But he missed his brother, so he hurried back into the dark room to free him, and as he approached, his shadow was projected on the wall, and the brother heard his voice and became afraid and murdered him.

The Professor closed the boy's diary, noting the title of the page he had just read: *My Father's Room.*

"It is just a dream," the boy said.

"Abrâr! The pious and righteous sun!" the Professor said, handing the small blue book back to the boy. "Not many get out to see her, and fewer still return to her warmth."

"What does this dream mean?" the boy asked.

"It is about the sun. Your dream is telling you to wake up and get yourself into the sun to see the truth."

"What truth?" the boy asked.

"The truth that will set you free. Or kill you."

"I am not inclined to take my own life," the boy said.

"Certainly not at this moment. But you might extinguish yourself while attempting to illuminate that part of you which refuses to be enlightened."

"I think the dream is about embarking on a journey," the boy replied. "The dream is telling me to escape my Father's room."

The Professor shook his head sadly.

"It is your room, not your Father's," was all he said.

PART ONE

Everyone called him Musa, Musa the Tâbi'een. It was not his given name, but the boy made no objection. Only Miriam, his Mother, called him by his given name, and only when she scolded him, which she would do when she discovered that he had slipped out into the night. It was past midnight, and he had ventured out for a secret walk in the snow, for the boy had a decision to make.

As he approached the stone mosque at the top of the hill, the wind kicked up and the icy snow stung his face. The mosque was dark but he proceeded, hoping the doors were open, for he had been walking a long time and he was cold, and though he no longer prayed or practiced salat, he wanted to sit and think about things before making his way back home. The boy lowered his head and stepped like a soldier, his black boots pushing the snow away like whitewater from the bow of a boat. He tripped once, where the road stopped and the grass lawn started, near the headstones. For sixteen years most Fridays he played on that grass while his Mother attended jumuah. No grass grew there now.

"Happy days gone," the boy reminded himself.

If the door was open, he decided, he would spend the night inside the mosque. Maybe then, he thought, some spirits or even his Mother's God might tell him what he should do.

He felt his heart thump under his coat as the cold iron handle moved. A gust with the strength of a sharqi pushed the heavy gray door out of his hand, and snowflakes danced into the room like dust, upslanting to the ash rafters then down again, as if expending their final moments in a joyous crescendo before falling to the pitch floor. The boy felt breezy whispers surround the room, voices outside of his head that issued welcomes and warnings all at once, and though he was in a mosque, he was frightened.

Right foot first, the boy ventured forth from the world of common snow and cold and into the shelter of supernatural wonder. Slowly and quietly he slipped inside the inky darkness, blindly reaching out with his hands as he walked. The room was familiar, even in the blackness. As a young boy, he had spent hours waiting in this very room; he knew every crack in the alabaster walls, he knew where the Priest's table protruded out, and he knew the length of the bookshelves that were filled with moldy books that the masjid worshippers no longer used but couldn't bear to discard. He reached out until his hands touched a wall and on it, a switch. Twelve lights, six on each wall, emitted a milky glow. They were designed to look like candles, but they were electric. The boy never liked the artificial lights; he believed that a mosque was a place where things should be genuine. But he was thankful for the electric lights tonight.

A stone pillar erupted near the minaret, a sable sentry beckoning him. A drab iron bowl, filled with water, rested on the rock. The boy bent over and touched his lips to the oily surface.

"Tastes like charcoal," he thought, remembering the days when his Father used to take him fishing and they would dip water out of the streams with citrus wood buckets. The water from those northern mountain woods tasted orange and green, like the trees and earth and rocks. The boy missed those days when his Father taught him how to dip the pail just so to avoid the leaves and skeeters. Now he just drank water from a metal faucet, like everyone else.

After a few more steps he stopped, removed his boots, brought his hands together and bowed. He rarely bowed so deeply before in the mosque, and he wondered what compelled him to do it now. The boy felt embarrassed, so he stopped and kneeled down on the worn carpet of the prayer room, but his legs were tight and he became uncomfortable, so he lay on his back and stared up into the intricate tile patterns of the dome. The boy started to recite his isha'ae, but could not recall the correct verses and he drifted off to sleep trying to remember them.

When he awoke, the snow was pressing against the windows like a hungry ghost. The dream didn't come, as he had hoped. He sighed and stared up at the dome, still awash in the muted heather light.

"That would be an omen, if I saw God's smile in the dome," he said, then scowled, realizing how stupid he was sounding. He watched as his breath floated up and vanished, then he rose like a corpse and walked about the prayer hall, scuffing his feet. One evening, long ago, he ventured into the masjid on a dare and wiped his shoes on the prayer mats, and was caught by the Priest.

"It is unwise to touch all that you can reach," was all the Priest said. The boy still wondered why the Priest did not scold him, or beat him like his Father did.

Digging his feet into the flat carpets now, alone in the dark mosque, the boy was reminded of both men: his Father who gave him flesh and blood, and the Priest who gave him courage to face his journey.

"I am my own father now," the boy thought, and he was right. Far off in the night a train horn sounded and the boy decided that he would listen to the dream, even though there were no signs in the mosque to convince him to do so. With resolve, he ventured back out into the storm.

As so the boy's hijrah began.

But the boy did not see the Priest, who was standing in the shadows in the back of the prayer hall, watching. For the Priest, the boy entering his mosque on a cold snowy night was the manifestation of his own dream, a dream that had haunted him since he was a boy, a dappled, dreary dream that he had never understood.

Until this night.

Winter came and went, yet still the boy had not answered his call, for he was unsure, and it was not until many months after the snow had melted and the southern sharqi winds came that the boy took action. He had been hoping that some force would intervene and erase his doubt. But he came to realize that there was no blackboard in the heavens upon which his name and purpose were neatly scribed, so he set out to write it himself.

"I am going away," the boy told his Mother one gray day.

He had to repeat his words; his Mother was busy cooking and moving iron pans around and could not hear very well. When she finally understood, she sat down at an unbalanced white table and cried.

"That is best for you, but I am sad about it," she said. "I don't want you to leave me, but I know I must let you go. It is time for your hijrah."

"The university is not far away, and I have been saving my money," the boy said, walking over to embrace her head.

"That is why you have been selling your old books," his Mother replied, ashamed. She had no money to give him. His Father had taken it all when he left.

"And some of my clothes," the boy added.

"Is it the dream again?" she asked, her smile pallid and tired. She did not like to talk about the boy's dreams, but the boy did, so she encouraged him and always listened, as a good Mother does.

"Yes. I have written it down, so I will not forget, in case it ever goes away."

"When will you leave?"

"Soon. We have some time together."

"Tell me again."

"If it pleases you," the boy replied.

After dinner they sat at the unbalanced white table and watched in silence as the smoke danced above the ash in the hearth. The boy knew that when his Mother stared into the blanched coals she was speaking to her God, her Allah, and though the boy was bored and restless, he did not interrupt her. The jinn, the creation of Allah made of smokeless fire, would not come to their table tonight.

When she was ready, she grabbed the boy's hands and clasped them together.

"Keep khabîth from my son, keep the evil and the wicked far from his face" she whispered, and the ivory charm that hung over her bleached neck bounced in agreement.

"Mother, I don't pray much these days," the boy confessed.

"Try."

And the boy turned in qiblah, his prayer direction, as if facing the Ka'ba. But he didn't feel comfortable about it. A black raven landed on the windowsill, and the boy wondered if his Mother's prayers were being paid attention somewhere far away, since though she called out often, her God, her Allah, did not seem to take much notice. After Father left, she was not allowed to go to the mosque. Her faith was curious to the boy, and it seemed so irrational after all they had been through, yet she still called out into the darkness.

"Dreams can be your reality. You know that, don't you, son?" she said and the bird flew off. "It is how the world communicates with us. Never ignore your dreams, for in the end, it is all we really have."

"She is trying to teach me religion again," the boy thought, but he did not interrupt her out of respect.

"Now tell me the dream about the dark girl again," his Mother asked.

The boy smiled.

"Last night it came again, as it has every night since Father left. I can see myself in a familiar room writing in my diary. In the room are stacks and stacks of books of many shapes and sizes. The covers are all different, some in tatters, some laced with jewels, some thick, some thin. But I seem to know what is written inside every one. As I am writing, a child appears and picks up a small book covered in leather and bound with wood. The child is very young, with dark skin and long flowing hair as black as night."

"An angel," his Mother said, though she knew it was a forbidden thought.

"Perhaps. She is only a child, so I am curious as to why she is studying the pages so intently, since she is not old enough to read."

"You learned to read when you were only five," his Mother said with a proud smile.

"Suddenly the child turns to a page and points to it and shouts: 'This is it!'" The boy paused and watched as his Mother's eyes brightened, as if gray ice had melted away to reveal the deep colors of the sea. She had heard the story a hundred times and always enjoyed the part where the dark child tells her son where to find his riches.

"Then, the child hands me the book," the boy continued, motioning with his arms, "and says to me: 'Here is where you will discover great wealth.' And she points to a page that has many numbers on it. As I reach for the book I lose track of the page, and when I look up to ask her to show me again, the child is gone, out of the window, into the night."

The woman sat quietly, thinking, but the boy knew what she was going to ask next. She had asked it a hundred times before.

"What did you see on that page?" she asked, interested as always.

"I could not read it. There were numbers, a ten and a thirteen I think, but I can never remember. There were some words too, but in a language I did not understand."

His Mother smiled. "I know what it means."

The boy fell back in laughter. Not once in six years had his Mother ever volunteered an explanation for the dream about the dark girl. "I am listening," he said with a grin.

"It is simple, really," she explained. "I am ashamed I never saw it before. It came to me, just now, when you told me you were leaving. The child in your dream is you, disguised as a girl instead of a boy. It is you pointing at your diary, which holds the secret to discovering your treasure. It is you pointing to words you cannot see, to a page that you cannot read. But I know what it means."

"What does it mean, Mother?"

"It means you need to understand the books; you must go to the university and learn to read."

"I know how to read already."

"Only some things can you read. That is a very important page, for it comes to you every night, and so you must learn how to read it. That is why you must go to the university. There you will learn. Son, your dream is a message from above, showing you The Way to find your wealth and happiness. You must go, because it is your destiny and you must follow it."

The fire had died out and the boy could feel the cold invading the room. He stared at the peppery coals in the hearth for a long while.

"I love you!" he said at last, and he hugged her.

That night, she sat by his bed for the last time.

"Mother, I am so tired of this same dream," he sighed. "Oh, it is a nice dream that helped me through a difficult time. But now I am going to the university, and I must put aside these childish dreams if I am to become a man."

"A physical man puts away childish dreams," she said, "but a transitional man embraces them with his heart and mind. Before anything happens, you first must dream and protect your dreams against all the world. Do not allow anyone, no matter how strong, no matter how convincing, to rob you of your dreams."

"Did you ever dream?" the boy asked.

The woman thought for a long time, and the boy could see she was smiling inside.

"I still do. When I was your age I had a very special dream, that I created the most wonderful gift in the world."

"What was it?"

"I would dream that one day I would have a child."

The boy smiled. "I guess your dream came true."

"Better than I ever imagined," and the woman smiled too.

"Good night, Mother."

"Good night, son."

It did not take long for the boy to fall asleep, because he wanted to dream about the dark girl who could point the way to his treasure. But that night, something about the girl had changed. She seemed more determined than ever to show him the page of the book she held in her hands, and he saw the numbers clearly, but still he could not understand them or determine their meaning.

It became the time when the sky turned fiery red at dusk, warning every creature that winter was on her way. As the leaves inked burgundy and gold on the mountain elms and citrus trees, the boy kept his mind occupied with work. Since the day his Father left the boy had earned a small wage at the hospital near the stone mosque, where the old worshippers would go to spend their last days. At first the Nurse would give the boy copper coins for sweeping the cherry wood floors, cleaning the leaves from the terra cotta gutters and washing the brick walkways that meandered around the headstones between the mosque where the worshippers would go to pray and the hospital where the worshippers would go to die. Over time the Nurse gave the boy more important jobs, and more coins. It was a good job, and he worked hard doing good things to help others who could not help themselves.

The boy enjoyed taking care of the patients most of all, and though the work was dull and demanded great patience, he enjoyed being needed. They called him 'Candy-Striper' because of the red-and-white-striped smock that he always wore, even when he tended to the rose bushes in the front, or redressed bandages when they became spotted with crimson stains.

The patients, especially the ones closest to death, liked having the boy nearby. "Candy-Striper, push me closer to the window," they would shout, or "Candy-Cane, cut my salmon," and the boy would dutifully assist. After many years he knew their needs and quirks as well as the Nurse did, and he would sing songs on their birthdays when nobody else would and attend their funerals when they passed on. He felt like a shepherd and the dying patients his flock, and knowing some things about the Koran and the Bible, this made him feel noble and important.

The Nurse was a short Albanian woman whose father and brother were painters. She was a mother to everyone in the hospital, laboring like a missionary whether she was emptying the bedpans or entering receipts into the maroon ledgers. The hospital was a sad place, for it was always perfumed in the smell of death, yet the Nurse smiled and smiled no matter the day or situation. Every time the old woman smiled it was as though she was offering a secret gift. She told the boy that a smile was the beginning of love, and this impressed the boy and he smiled often too, which balanced the death and pain that surrounded him.

On the last day of his employ at the hospital, after he unsuccessfully attempted his fajr, the boy told the Nurse about his dream. She folded her hands on her red apron and listened with great intent. When he finished he felt embarrassed, and wished he had not told her.

"It's a small thing, really. Quite silly, don't you think?" he said when she was quiet.

"Keep faith in the small things," the Nurse replied, "for that is where your strength lies, and you will need every bit of strength for your journey."

"I will miss this place, and the love you give these people," the boy said. "I wish I knew how to give such extraordinary love, as you do."

"Genuine love does not need to be extraordinary," the Nurse smiled. "Just love others without getting tired."

"Even Hussein?" the boy asked. "He is so mean to you, yet you love him like your own child."

The woman reached back and ran her hand through her long chestnut hair, as if fixing to braid it. "Every one of them is Mohammad in disguise," she said, "each one on a journey of incredible power and purpose, and like you, each on their way, each following their own brick road to the place they need to be."

Outside, a red-wattled plover landed on a tree branch and perched like a red and white hat suspended over a wooden rafter. The boy watched as it called out three times, searching for its mate, before fluttering off.

"Most certainly a sign," the boy thought, but he did not know what it meant.

"That bird is no Ilâh. Or is it?" the Nurse posed, reading the boy's mind. "Is that simply a birdsong she sings, or is it a khutbah, a sermon crafted only for your ears? Listen, boy. Is she she telling you to be on the look out for helpers and teachers along The Way? You will need them, just as they will need you."

"But how will I know when I meet them?" the boy asked.

"You won't," she replied. "That's the fun part. Everyone wears a disguise. But here's a little trick." She leaned in close. The boy could smell her now, a foreign odor of sweet lavender and rust, like the herbs the Priest burned in the mosque. Then the Nurse smiled her wide smile.

Nothing more, just a smile.

And the boy smiled back and stood up, and as he did his red-and-white-striped apron caught on the chair and ripped.

"Come now, it is time to gather your flock," the woman smiled.

"It is too early for dinner," the boy said.

"Yes, but everyone wants to see you one last time. Even Hussein."

"I don't know what to say to everyone," the boy gasped, terrified of having to give a speech.

"Just stand there, and if you can't speak to thirty people, then speak to just one," the Nurse replied.

The boy scowled. Sometimes the old woman didn't make any sense. Her words always presented a paradox, and he never fully understood what she meant by them. She would say that if you loved until it hurt, there would be no more hurt, only love.

"One day I will return from the university to see my flock," he thought, "and I will know much more of the world and what her words mean."

As the people gathered, the Nurse could see that the boy was nervous.

"We are all pencils in the hand of God," she said, trying to reassure him. "Just say what you have already written within your heart. Say that you are leaving because you have found The Way, and as you follow it, the entire world will conspire to help you."

"I hope so," the boy sighed, "for I am about to start to search for my riches."

"Oh, you started long ago," the Nurse replied. "But as you pursue these riches you speak of, always beware of the poverty that awaits you."

"What poverty?" the boy asked.

"Being alone, feeling unwanted. Look about this room, and gaze upon your flock. Do you not see the disease of loneliness? No amount of money will pull you out of such poverty. On your journey, do not become nobody to anybody. Be somebody to everybody."

"I promise," the boy replied. He was not worried. He had always been alone and he enjoyed his independence, and he knew that once he found his treasure he would not be lonely. "And I promise that when I return, I will buy you a television for the sitting room."

"No matter how much money you may give away, it will not be enough," the Nurse said sadly. "You are here now, and your being here has been so much more important than money. You have loved us, with your heart. Keep your money, but always give us your love."

"Of course I will," the boy said, "and once I succeed, I will return."

"The universe doesn't require you to succeed. It only requires that you try."

The boy and the Nurse looked up and saw that the people had already assembled and had heard their conversation, and those that could smiled and nodded in agreement, and they all shared in laughter. The boy said some words and found that they came easily, for they came directly from his heart. Then the Nurse walked to the corner of the room, to fetch her mandolin.

"Now let us sing some songs for our little khalafee, our brave traveler," she said, "starting with one I have written for this very occasion. It's just a little thing."

"There is great strength in little things," the boy said, and realized that his last day with his flock was like a joyous hand and a sad hand clasping as one.

On the walk home that evening the boy stared up at the red sky and the red sun sinking into the horizon in the direction of the university and he fought his tears, for he knew that many in his flock would pass away before he would return, and he would never see them again.

The university sessions started at the end of summer, when the pumpkins were bulging fat and deep orange, but the boy had not registered. The university was far away, and the boy had spent all of his savings for tuition and board and did not have enough money for a bus ticket. His Father agreed to drive him in his truck, but only when it was convenient. And so the boy waited six days.

His father was one of the kâfirûn, one of the disbelievers.

On the seventh day his Father drove up in a battered white truck with large titian letters that read: "Imran's Plumbing and Heating." The boy had carefully painted the letters on the truck years before, though he was not paid for it. As a child he had played in the truck, but today the boy simply slid onto the front seat beside his Father and pressed against the metal passenger door, as if a trine wedged itself between them and the umbra required much space. High above, the boy's Mother lifted the sullied window in her apartment and waved, and the pigeons fluttered away, but the boy did not see them or his Mother.

"Hungry?" the man in the truck asked. He offered the boy an apricot, but the boy shook his head and looked away and watched as mountains and towns with their busy people passed them by. As they turned onto the wider road, the sharqi wind blew violently through the windows and pulled the boy's favorite hat off his head and out of the truck, but his Father did not stop to retrieve it.

Out of boredom, the boy pulled his diary out of his pack and brushed off the faded blue cover, as if the small book were a priceless artifact.

"What's that?" his Father asked.

"Something I wrote a long time ago," the boy said as he began to read, pretending to be deep in thought.

"I don't know how to write," the man replied, trying to strike up a conversation, but the boy said nothing, for he felt nothing, and did not feel like talking.

"Sure wish I could write," the man said. "Must make you happy to write, and let people read what you wrote."

The boy thought this comment odd. His Father never spoke about happiness.

"So you're going to get educated," the man continued. "Couldn't get me to go to that place, not in a million years. See, plumbers don't need those books. I did some asking around, and you know something? Not one Journeyman in town ever set foot in that university. Perfectly good waste of money, if you ask me."

"I didn't ask you," the boy replied.

"Then I guess you will not be a plumber."

The boy's stomach tightened. "I never wanted to be a plumber," he replied, wondering if he had angered his Father, but the man simply nodded in agreement.

"Such laghw from such a little man! Plumbing doesn't want you," he said. "It takes certain skills to be a plumber. See son, what you never understood was, being a plumber is the most worthy profession one could ever dream to have."

The boy mustered up his courage. Ordinarily he would not have spoken up, for fear of a beating, but he was older now and going off to the university to become a man, and since his Father was driving, he could not slap at him easily.

"What did you ever do with your life?" the boy challenged.

"Easy," the man snorted. "I made you. A son. That is my greatest accomplishment, the thing I am the proudest of."

"You are acting strange," the boy replied.

"Get ready for it, for you are about to enter a cave where people will be acting strange, and you will see many strange things. The world is not always what it seems. Take me, for instance. A bad Father? Yes, I give you that. But I am a good man. Your Mother knows this."

"Don't talk about Mother," the boy threatened, his face hot. The boy wanted the road to end and the university to appear. He did not like listening to his Father talk about such things.

"Still love her, your Mother, that is. Surprises you, doesn't it? We all have wounds. Wounds are a part of life, in fact, wounds create life. When a man penetrates a woman it is an invasion, it makes a wound in the woman, and that wound creates life, just as we created you. Like sand that invades an oyster, causing pain, creating the pearl. It is from these wounds that we heal and create. That is life."

"I do not understand why you are talking such nonsense," the boy said, and he truly didn't.

"Do you know why I became a plumber?" his Father continued. "Because of my father. When I was young and he was angry, he would beat me with a thick iron pipe. That pipe would leave orange and purple bruises all over my back. But I loved my father. I couldn't blame him, so I blamed the pipe, and I swore that I wouldn't let that pipe control me or beat me, not ever again. I learned everything I could about pipes...how they are made, how they fit together. I learned how to bend them and cut them and connect them. Before long the pipe became my slave, and I became its master. Now it works for me, not against me."

"People in town say you are the best plumber around," the boy volunteered. He was a kind boy, even though he did not love his Father so much.

"Being a plumber healed my wounds," the man continued. "It gave me life, but it created new wounds. The Circle of Fatherhood does not start and stop. For every beginning there is an end, and each end starts a new beginning. Plumbing is hard work and I was always working, always away from you and your Mother. When I was tired and your Mother was busy with you, I took up with another woman. It was a mistake, but I do not regret it."

"Why do you tell me all this now?" the boy asked. "That was long ago."

"Because now's the time for you to hear it," the man said, staring off into the road. "It's by no strange coincidence that when a man finally sees that his Father was right, he's got a son who's convinced he's wrong. It's the Circle of Fatherhood."

The boy did not understand this discussion about the Circle of Fatherhood. He was going off to the university, not going off to raise children. He decided to keep quiet, hoping the conversation would end, but his Father would not allow it.

"The Circle of Fatherhood has certain truths. One is that my wound and your wound are one in the same. I hope you can learn from it, as I'm learning from you. Do you know I carry a picture of you in my wallet, where I used to carry my money?"

"You never hit me with a pipe," the boy said, looking over at his Father for the first time. But the boy remembered the beatings. His Father would strike him with his belt, or throw hard things at him. Once a book hit him in the face and his eye swelled to the size of an apricot with a blind pit inside. The boy could not see for forty days and nights.

"But I did other things," the man confessed. "Now you must become your own Father, as I did. When you have children some day, you'll love 'em, sure enough. But you'll create wounds from which they must heal. That's what we're meant to do. That's the Circle of Fatherhood."

The boy did not answer, for he realized that he didn't know his Father very well, and this worried him. At last the truck stopped and the engine puked smoke and sputtered itself into silence. As the boy was getting out, the man reached behind the seat and retrieved an amber-colored envelope.

"You'll come back home, sooner than you expect," his Father said. "You won't find whatever you seek inside these orange brick buildings, and you'll run home scared and desperate, and knowing you, you'll be asking me for work. Perhaps you'll become a plumber, like me. Wouldn't surprise me in the slightest, because the world's a dangerous and unforgiving place. But since there's a small chance you won't ever come back, you should take this. It ain't worth much, but it's all I got." He handed the boy the envelope.

"What is it?" the boy asked as he inspected the certificate tucked inside.

"A man sold it to me; promised that one day it'd be worth lots of money," his Father sighed. "But today it is worth very little. Sorry, it's all I have to give, but it's all you really need."

"I could have used the money for tuition," the boy said as he pulled his rucksack over his shoulder and waved good-bye.

"Promise me one thing," his Father shouted out. "If you do follow your dream, and claim these riches you seek, then you'll have accomplished something most men do not. And when you do discover that treasure, promise me that you'll take care of your Mother. That's the most important duty of all."

The boy turned. Orange and yellow leaves fell from the shady trees and pooled at his black boots. "Don't you want anything?" the boy asked.

"No," his Father replied. "You've given me all I ever wanted."

The boy turned and walked, kicking up the leaves. He heard the truck engine ignite, and he wanted to turn and see the titian letters he had painted long ago, but he did not want to see his Father's face, for he knew that he would not see his Father again.

"But if I do, I am certain I will see him differently," the boy thought to himself, holding the amber envelope as he entered the tall gates to start his journey.

PART TWO

The boy was eager to learn about history and literature and philosophy and economics, but such sessions were filled by students who had arrived early. So the boy was told to enroll in other courses that were not popular, such as thermodynamics and chemistry and calculus and physics. He was not very good at math, and he did not enjoy science very much, but he had already given the university all his money, so he was forced to study what they had left to offer.

The boy found the classes difficult, so he spent all of his time in the library, reading thick scientific books with yellowed pages that smelled of cheese and straw. He soaked up all he could, holding it inside his head like a sponge, because he did not want to fail and have to face his Father again. Consequently he did not meet many people or befriend other students, for his singular path was to learn and succeed in his classes.

The Maulâ, whom everyone called simply the Librarian, a man of foreign descent who went by the name of Mister Campbell, noticed that that boy was always in the library when other students were playing about, and how the boy took great care of the delicate, yellowed books. Over time the Librarian introduced himself, and some evenings, after the library was closed, he would tell the boy grand stories of Indians who dressed like flying monkeys and vengeful Greek goddesses and tribes of savages who lived in banana leaf huts and worshipped the sun. The Librarian offered the boy a job cleaning the books and mending the bindings, for which the boy received a small wage. The boy was grateful, for he was increasingly hungry and his money was running out, and he enjoyed Mister Campbell's tales.

Sometimes the Librarian discarded old books that the students had torn or damaged, and the boy would retrieve them and stack them in his room and read them late at night. He enjoyed spending time in the company of authors such as Homer and Shakespeare and Dante and Steinbeck, and he learned more from Mister Campbell's books than he did from the teachers. Thomas Paine taught him about the American Revolution and Adam Smith taught him about economics and Albert Einstein taught him about energy. Some books gave him great amusement, especially those about men who had lost their way, who were confused about their journey but still pressed on. Like Don Quixote, who spent his time needing to destroy something he thought was evil, only at the end to learn that he was hunting something harmless, or Crane's young boy who didn't believe he should be a hero but eventually became one. He didn't like the story about Pip who was poor and still ends up poor at the end, or the one about the old fisherman who finally lands a big fish that is eaten by sharks, so the old man goes home and dies, but generally the boy enjoyed the stories of men finding their way in the world.

One autumn day the boy took a long walk through the university grounds, watching as the yellow leaves kicked up from his black boots like the snow used to do. He sat down on a bronze bench in the shadow of the masjid to study his chemical equations, but his eyes sunk like yokes and he could not keep them open, for the sun was warm and the lesson was quite dull.

An old man in a cream-colored suit approached, shooed a bird off the armrest and sat on the bench. He had flowing alabaster hair parted down the middle of his large head, and a thick white mustache tucked under his sundial nose.

"A little early to be testing for atomics, isn't it?" the old man asked as he lit up a fat cigar with an official gold ring wrapped around one end.

"The classes I wanted were all taken," the boy politely replied, "so they told me to study science."

"Another seeker confined by his own minhaj. We told you to do that? Never trust this place, especially the teachers."

"And who are you to say such a thing?" the boy asked, offended.

The old man coughed. "Oh, one of the teachers. Been holding court here since before you were born. Around here they call me the Old Professor, when they think I can't hear them. But I can."

The boy introduced himself. "You said never trust teachers, but your fellow teachers have me studying sodium and the yellow rings of Saturn; they promised me that if I become an engineer, I will make a lot of money."

The Professor snorted and the sweet smell of saffron tobacco rose above them. "Did we teachers tell you that we make more money when students like you pay for classes you don't want? Bet we didn't tell you that!"

"Of course not," the boy replied.

"You think the world owes you a living, do you?" the Professor asked. "So that is why you are here, to make lots of money?"

"Yes," the boy replied. "Then I can give money to my Mother and buy a television for the hospital. And when I have children, they won't have to worry about money one bit."

"Money, money, money. Not much of a cause, is it?"

"You are a teacher, so by your own words, I should not trust you," the boy replied, feeling witty.

"How true," the Professor replied, smacking his chest with his fist. "But you should at least listen, because everything that is taught to you by teachers is taught from the outside going in. Learning takes place from the inside going out. Trust yourself, not those who say they should be trusted. Everyone has something to say, but you need to choose what you should hear."

The Professor spoke in circles, like the old Nurse. The words were the words of Ghaib, the Great Unseen. So the boy did not reply. He stared into his book, pretending to read, since he did not want to talk to the old man. The Professor whistled like a canary to amuse himself, and filled the air with the bisque smoke from his cigar. The boy was preparing to gather his rucksack and take leave when the old man cleared his throat.

"You need a better cause than money, my friend," the Professor said as he rolled the cigar around on his lips.

"It is my cause, and I accept it," the boy replied.

"No doubt you do," the Professor replied, happy for conversation. "I suppose a man cannot live his life without his own approval. But you are no different than the other young people who come here just hoping to make money. Or are you? Are you perceptive enough to witness the grand lie, the lie that has walked the lawns of this university thirteen times before the truth has had a chance to get out of bed and lace its shoes?"

"It is not a lie. Money can get you many things," the boy replied.

"Perhaps, but it is the wrong reason to be coming here. You should come to a place like this to discover The Way."

"What is The Way?" the boy asked.

"You tell me," the Professor replied.

"I don't understand you at all," the boy said, wondering if the strange man in the sandy suit was really a teacher.

"Why did you come to this place?" the man asked. "And don't tell me it's about money."

The boy was embarrassed; he did not want to say. But the boy was lonely and he enjoyed the sweet smell of tobacco, and he was curious about the old man. So the boy told the Professor his dream about the dark girl, and how it was an omen that drove him to seek his riches by becoming educated. When he finished, the Professor smiled, and the tips of his thick ivory mustache inched up and touched his earlobes.

"You remember it so well!" he exclaimed. "And it is such a wonderful dream; so rich in allegory."

"What is allegory?" the boy asked.

"In one sense, allegory is everything we see and experience. In these stone buildings here, it means a representation of abstract thoughts using characters or events. But I am too simple for that, so I call it story-telling. But don't worry about the word, for what matters is The Way."

"The Way?" the boy repeated.

"This dream of yours is a signpost, pointing where you need to go. Each of us has a path to take; we all seek The Way. The hard part is to have the courage to follow The Way once we find it. Often it takes a dream to wake us up."

The boy thought for a moment. "I suppose, since my dream brought me here to become an engineer."

"That is one interpretation," the Professor replied. "It may have even brought the two of us together on this bench, under the shadow of the masjid on this fine day. But the real question is, where is it guiding you next?"

"To be an engineer, to make a lot of money building things."

"Do you know why?" the Professor asked.

"My Father was a plumber who never learned to write," the boy said, his voice calm. A swallowtail butterfly flew nearby and landed on the bench, but seemed bothered by the cigar smoke and fluttered off. The boy continued: "After my Father left my Mother, I vowed never to be a plumber. I wanted to be educated, to read and understand complicated words and numbers, as an engineer does. Engineers write plans and build things like skyscrapers and machines and airplanes. I will be better than my Father, and I will build great things and be the best engineer in the world."

The Professor nodded his head in approval. "Good show, son!" he said. "That is a more noble cause than pursuing money. But it is not The Way."

"It is for today," the boy replied.

"The Way is for today, yesterday, and tomorrow. It is for every day of your existence. It does not change, and you cannot change it. It simply is."

"What classes do you teach here?" the boy asked.

"I teach from the works of the salaf," the Professor replied solemnly. "My lessons concern the works of Aristotle, Plato, Mohammad, Descartes, the Matazilites, Nietzsche, and other folks."

"Philosophy. One day I will take your class."

"I prefer the term salafi. When the student is ready, the teacher appears."

"I promise I will," the boy replied.

"What adab, what manners! Better a broken promise than one never made. That is a start."

"You don't trust me?"

"I trust you plenty; it is you who does not trust you. When you learn to trust yourself, then others will follow you. But don't wait to take my class to learn the most important lesson."

"And what lesson is that?" the boy asked.

The Professor leaned in close, as if he was sharing a guarded secret.

"Always sail away from the safe harbor. Years from now, when you are all grown and wise, you will be more saddened by what you didn't do than by what you did do. You are a dreamer, boy. That's the first step. But to dream and remain comfortable in bed is no life worth living. You must take the second and third steps."

"What are those?" the boy asked.

"Next, you must be a believer," the man replied. "You must be ready to hear the answer, and trust me, the universe will respond to whatever you ask for."

"And the third step after that?"

The Professor stood up suddenly, his white hair falling around his face like a buttery halo. He smiled at the boy and walked away from the bench, kicking up the yellow leaves, pulling the tobacco air away with him as he strolled. As the boy watched the old man shuffle off, he was reminded of what the Nurse had said, that everyone was Mohammad in disguise. He wondered if the Professor was one of the old mentors she had warned him about.

"Crazy old fool," the boy decided. "I wish he would have told me the third step instead of playing this game with me."

All at once, far across the lawn, the Professor spun around on his heels in front of a row of sunflowers.

"You must receive!" the Professor cried out, reaching his hands up to the sun and repeating the phrase three times. He laughed a loud, delightful laugh and shouted "salâmu-'alaikum" three times. The students walking about looked over at him and whispered amongst themselves.

The boy returned to his chemistry book, the bird returned to the bench, and it did not take long for the boy to forget about the Professor completely.

☼

The boy studied very hard at the university. He never left, not even during the summer or for religious holidays, for he so much wanted to do well his studies, and besides he had no money for travel. For three years he labored in his classes and in the library, and he learned much about complex subjects such as kinetics and quantum theory and magnetic attraction. But because he spent his days and nights in books, he did not make many friends. He didn't mind of course, for he was a solitary person, like a shepherd or a fisherman.

One day the Librarian was visited by a young student and the two talked for a long time, and then ventured outside for a stroll in the empty field outside the library windows. The Librarian just kept walking and talking, discussing what seemed like important matters with the student. The boy thought this odd, because the Librarian never went for walks and rarely spoke to students, except to help them find books.

Suddenly the Librarian was waving, motioning to the boy to come outside, and the student was jumping up and waving his hands in the air, as if shooing crows off of high stalks of corn. The boy could see they were both smiling, and as he approached the student leapt forward, hand extended.

"My name is Tamir. I've heard a lot about you," the student said. He looked strange to the boy; he had thick blond hair that clung to the top of his head like straw and skin that was tan and porous like canvas.

"Not likely," the boy replied. "Not many know much about me."

The Librarian smiled. "Tamir will be working with you in the stacks. I am certain you two boys will get along swimmingly."

"I love swimming!" Tamir shouted, and the Librarian rolled his eyes and left them alone in the field.

"You don't look like you need the money," the boy said, noting how neat Tamir's clothes were tailored.

"It is not about the money," Tamir replied as they walked back to the library. "My dad insists that I work, so that I may appreciate what work is like. And what better place to work than among the smartest people to have ever lived!"

The boy thought this odd, because he needed to work, since his Father had left him and his Mother was very poor. Work was neither a lesson nor an activity to appreciate.

"I chose the library because my dad is smart, so much smarter than I'll ever be," Tamir continued. "He went to this university long ago, and gave money to construct this building, so he arranged with Mister Campbell to have me work here with you. I am hoping these books will rub off on me. See, I'm not the sharpest tool on the farm, but I know that if I only had a brain, my dad would love me much more."

"Long ago I could not read and my Father could. Now I can write but my Father cannot," the boy volunteered.

"You are lucky. My dad is one of the smartest men in the world," Tamir replied.

"I am sure you are much smarter than you know, and all you need is a little self-confidence."

"I like you already," Tamir crowed, grabbing the boy's hand and shaking it rapidly. "Let's have something to eat, you and me, and I want to learn all about you."

"First we have to organize the reference catalogs," the boy said, trying to sound authoritative. "See the gilded letters on those three cabinets? You organize the two labeled A-G and H-N, and I'll take the last one labeled O-Z."

"I am looking forward to being your Journeyman," Tamir said as they went to work.

☼

Winter came and went, followed by spring. One warm day, as the boys were applying lotion to the bisque-leather bindings that protected the maps, Tamir spied a small blue book peeking out of the boy's tattered rucksack.

"What's this?" Tamir asked as he grabbed it and ran off, and the boy took to the chase around the stacks until the Librarian noticed and sent them both home.

"What's in that envelope?" Tamir asked when he finally returned the boy's diary.

"A certificate of a company, from my Father," the boy replied. "It's not worth anything."

"You never know about such papers, my brother," Tamir replied. "You might be carrying treasure in your sack. My dad could tell you; every year on my birthday he gives me a certificate."

"Is he a plumber?" the boy asked.

"Heaven's no," Tamir laughed. "He works for a bank, far away from here, and he will know what your certificate is worth. He is coming to fetch me soon to take me up to our lake house in Muskoka. Why don't you come with me, and spend the summer with me at the lake? It would be great fun."

The boy was delighted, but he knew he could not leave his job in the library.

"Thank you, but I cannot," the boy said sadly. "I need to work so that I have enough money for next year. For me work is not a lesson; it is my livelihood, and without it I would have to leave the university."

Tamir nodded, but his eyes remained bright. "But you could work at the lake house! My dad has more jobs than you could possibly complete: there are leaves to rake and fences to paint and boats to clean, and he will pay you more than old man Campbell does. You and I could have a grand summer together. It is a wonderful plan."

The boy could not decide, and for the next six days and nights he tossed in his bed. A significant choice was before him, and he wished he had some device or omen to guide him towards what he should do. But he had no such tools, and no omens came to visit. He studied his dreams for clues, every bit and piece he could envision, but they offered no answers.

"What is the right path?" he asked over and over in the darkness. He knew his path was to become an engineer and make money, but to achieve that, he had to stay at the university and work in the library. The Way was laid before him; the boy simply had to take the steps. But the opportunity to spend the summer with Tamir in a faraway place was a gift, something that would never present itself again.

Deep inside the boy believed he should reward himself, leave the safe harbor of the Librarian and the university and set sail into uncharted waters. Tamir had described his home and Muskoka so many times that the boy could envision the boathouses and servant quarters and master estate rising above the shimmering lake like an emerald city. He could fish and swim with Tamir on some days and do chores on others. Tamir was right, it was a wonderful plan, but it would take him off his path, and put his studies at great risk, and so the boy was torn.

"It is not easy to choose The Way," the boy sighed.

A few days later he gave Tamir his decision. Tamir jumped high into the air and danced a floppy jig in delight, right in the library, and the other students looked at him and rolled their eyes, and the Librarian sent them both home, as he had done before.

But the boys did not mind, for they laughed and rejoiced knowing they would be spending the entire summer together in Muskoka.

✸

The next day they boarded a small plane that Tamir's dad, the Banker, flew himself. The boy had seen planes soar high above in the sky but had never been in one, and he was afraid.

"This is how a bird must live," the boy wondered as they embarked. "Freedom brings so much fear." The boy felt green and sick inside, and Tamir tried to put him at ease by playing cards, and eventually the boy grew accustomed to the experience by gazing out at the clouds and the patches of sage forests and grassy plains and terraced farms that passed below, and fell fast asleep.

"There it is," the Banker announced many hours later. Below, shimmering like jade, were hundreds of lakes, and lakes within lakes, and islands within islands, as if a giant creature had jumped down from the moon and danced about in the green mud.

"Muskoka is over a billion years old," the Banker continued. "The rocks you see here were once the initial crust of the planet. The Indians who lived here long ago named this place Mesqua Ukee, which means 'not easily turned back in the day of battle.'

After the Indians came the explorers, then the missionaries, then the miners and the machinery barons. Now it is owned by intellectual men, bankers and academics and such, who appreciate the beauty and value of this land. One wonders who will come next, to claim this beauty from the intellectuals."

"Perhaps transitional men," the boy whispered, "who are timeless and do not take control of the land, but rather become one with it."

"You sound like the Algonquin," Tamir whispered back, and the Banker frowned, so the boys went to playing cards until the trip ended.

Once on land the entourage was taken to a wooden motor boat which carried them across a large lake to a small island. The property was green and lush, surrounded by jack pine, spruce, tamarack, balsam, white birch and poplar trees. The houses were larger than the boy had ever seen, especially the main house, which was bigger than the stone mosque and the Nurse's hospital combined.

"Paradise," the boy thought.

"Welcome to Squirrel Island," the Banker said to the boy once they unpacked. He was an older gentleman, corn-fed and jolly in appearance, with tussled gray hair and thick black glasses. He was drinking a soda and offered the boy one. "Nothing better in this world than Coca-Cola in a green glass bottle," the Banker said.

"Thank you," the boy replied. "This is a beautiful place you have here, sir."

The Banker nodded. "I've been fortunate…made some money from companies in textiles and insurance, that sort of thing. Tell me, what do you want to be when you graduate, son?"

The boy had to think, for now the answer was not as obvious. "At first I wanted to be an engineer, but after meeting Tamir and you, perhaps I should be a stock picker."

The Banker laughed. "You make it sound like I'm in the corn fields, pulling ears off the stalks! I'd rather call myself an investor in valuable companies. I don't pick stocks, I pick companies, and when I find one I like, I give it my money, with the hope that the company over time will give me more back."

"Lots of people do that," the boy replied, "but lose their money."

"My formula is different," the Banker replied. "Anyone can make money if the market is rising. But when the tide goes out, you can see who is swimming naked."

The boy wasn't sure what the Banker was saying, for there was no such market in his province, but he wanted to learn more, for it was clear the Banker had become extremely wealthy in his work.

"Sir, I am searching for my destiny," the boy said. "All my life I have been haunted by a dream, a dream which has led me to the university to be an engineer. By following this dream, I believe I will make money, and I would like to know how to invest it, so that I never have to worry about money ever again."

"First, tell me about this dream," the man asked. And the boy did, and the Banker smiled knowingly, as if it were a familiar story.

"I cannot interpret your dream, but I can tell you how to be a good investor," the Banker said. "You only need to remember three rules. The first rule is to never lose."

"What's the second rule?" the boy asked.

"Never forget the first rule," the Banker smiled.

"And the third?"

The Banker took a long sip on his soda, then said: "There are three kinds of people in this world: those who can count, and those who can't."

The boy laughed politely. He thought the Banker was funny, but not very helpful. The man sensed this and straightened his back.

"But there are other things you should know about banking," he continued. "Always keep your reputation carefully guarded. It takes a lifetime to build one, but only a few minutes to lose it."

"That's what the Librarian says."

"A smart man, that Campbell. If past history was all there was to the game, the richest people would be librarians."

"And bankers," the boy said, "but probably not engineers. I wonder if I should be a banker like you some day, living in a far away city. But the teachers say I shouldn't."

"Be careful about letting teachers interfere with your education," the Banker replied. "I am sure they will say that engineering is the best path for you, but a public-opinion poll is no substitute for good old-fashioned thinking."

The boy thought it odd, that his Mother had said the same thing.

The next day the boy approached the Banker as he was swinging in his hammock, sipping another soda. The boy pulled out the company certificate from his diary and presented it.

"What's that?" the Banker asked, pointing at the boy's book.

"An old diary," the boy said. "I used to write down my dreams every night. I don't do that any more, of course."

"Why not?" the Banker asked.

"Because I want to be a man and men don't scribble down their dreams at night."

The Banker shook his head. "Son, being a man is all about understanding and accepting your dreams."

This made the boy uncomfortable and he didn't want to talk about dreams again.

"Can you tell me if this certificate is valuable?" he asked, changing the subject.

"I am no oracle, but I know of this company," the Banker replied. "If a business does well, the paper eventually follows. But right now this business is not doing well. It will take a miracle to turn this company around."

"Should I hold onto it?" the boy asked.

"Seems that's what you have been doing so far, so why change your strategy?" the Banker advised. "You should only own paper in a company that you'd be perfectly happy holding if the market shut down for many, many years. My favorite holding period is forever, for when you find a good Entrepreneur with a good company, you will find a great certificate worth holding."

"What is an Entrepreneur?" the boy asked, sad that the certificate was not worth anything.

The Banker pushed back his chair and gazed out over the lake as a yellow steamship chugged along the opposite shore. "An Entrepreneur is what an Entrepreneur does," he explained. "The person is the function; the function the person. Could be anybody…a merchant, a teacher, a scientist…anyone at all. Jesus was an Entrepreneur, so was Buddha, so was Muhammad, perhaps not in the market sense as we define it today, but they were Entrepreneurs nonetheless: people who believed in something bigger than themselves and pulled together the resources to achieve their vision. They were innovators who organized the world around them to take advantage of an opportunity and make something happen."

"I hope to meet an Entrepreneur one day," the boy said.

"I am certain you already have," the Banker replied. "A Priest who raises money to build a mosque, he is an Entrepreneur. A woman who starts a hospital for the sick and dying is an Entrepreneur. A man who learns a trade and hires himself out as a Journeyman, he too is an Entrepreneur."

"My father is a plumber. He drives his own truck," the boy replied.

"Then you, my friend, are the son of an Entrepreneur!" the Banker said, slapping the boy on the back. "Anyone who is a personification of the market process is, by definition, an Entrepreneur. They come in all shapes and sizes, from all backgrounds, but they all have one thing in common."

"What is that?" the boy asked.

The Banker smiled. "The Entrepreneur leads in the world by following his bliss."

✿

The next morning the boy was sitting on the dock in front of the main house, flapping his feet in the cool Muskoka waters and watching the geese fly, when the Banker approached with some unfortunate news. The boy's certificate was not worth anything, for the company had come under financial hardship.

"Tuck it away and check again in a few years," the Banker instructed. "These are difficult times, and the fate of companies, like people, can change dramatically."

The boy walked away, his head low, not wanting the Banker to see his face. He had long fantasized that the certificate was an omen, and if it were worth something, then perhaps that meant he should become a banker. But it was not to be, yet what worried the boy most was that he realized in his heart that he did not want to be an engineer. He had hoped that the child in his dream pointing at a page with numbers was pointing at a certificate, but since the certificate was worthless, the boy now doubted himself.

He spent the rest of the morning sitting on the bunky over the boathouse, confused and fallow. He had dutifully followed his dream to the university, but he had stepped off his intended path by spending a summer of leisure at the lake. Perhaps, the boy thought, his straying from The Way was the reason the dream decided to fail him. He felt his future come crashing down, and he was truly lost.

Eventually Tamir found the boy, and sensing something was wrong, devised a plan to cheer him up.

"Let's go on an adventure across the lake, to see the Algonquin," Tamir said.

"The Tâghût? Is that permitted?"

Tamir nodded. And so they packed a canoe with green apples and olives and ventured in a canoe over the water, with Tamir steering from the back. Tamir explained that the one in the rear sets the course, not the one in the front, and the boy pondered the mechanics of the phenomenon, as an engineer would. The two friends paddled for a long time. As they approached the shore on the opposite end of the lake, a small opening appeared between the mossy boulders and crowded trees.

"This is Algonquin land," Tamir whispered as they penetrated the blackness. They navigated up a stream and past a thundering waterfall that kissed their skin with moist, sticky lips. The stream narrowed, and a stadium of sweet maple collapsed above them, blocking out the sun, and the island forest grew still.

"If we are lucky, Sibyl is here today," Tamir whispered.

"Who is Sibyl?" the boy asked, but Tamir did not answer, and the boy was growing fearful and considered that it was better if he did not know.

Gradually the boys' eyes adjusted to the plum darkness. As they pressed on, they could see that many of the taller trees were bare. On a large dead branch, a black hawk stared down upon them and squawked. Tamir threw an apple and the bird launched and sailed away, and the boys shared a nervous laugh.

Eventually the stream became too wretched to paddle so they tied the canoe to a limb and set out on foot. The thicket pressed down upon them and the trees drooped overhead, forming a dark tunnel through which the boys made their way. Wet feathery ferns erupted from the evergreen ground, soaking their skins, and the humid air was difficult to breathe, but still Tamir pushed forward and the boy followed close behind.

"There it is," Tamir whispered. In a clearing ahead the boy spied a small cabin made of wood and hide. Eggs, mostly broken, were scattered about the dirt yard, and there were chickens pecking near the cabin door.

"The Algonquin lives here," Tamir said.

"Is this a friendly place?" the boy asked.

"Depends," a voice erupted from the clearing. "Whether a place is friendly or hostile is entirely up to you." An old woman appeared from behind the cabin. "Hello, Etchemin," she shouted.

"It is the Indian name she gave me," Tamir whispered. "It means canoe man, because I come to see her in a canoe."

"This boy is here to see Powwaw?" the old woman demanded, but Tamir simply shook his head, for he knew not what the woman meant. The boy wanted to turn and leave; he did not like the place.

"He is my friend," Tamir said, "and I wanted him to meet you."

The woman approached the boy. She raised her arms and swooped towards him suddenly, pressing her palms against the boy's head. The boy fell to the ground, his forehead smeared in oily black soot. The pungent odor made his nose and eyes leak.

"I will call you Annawon," the old woman shouted. "Now you may sit by my fire. Gather some eggs and bring your apples, and we will have a feast."

"What did you put on me?" the boy demanded, as Tamir hunted around the cabin for eggs.

The Algonquin spoke. "Many years ago, winter in these woods was a difficult time. Firewood was scarce, so the Etchemin would not bathe for many months. But still the Etchemin would go to their tiny church across the lake. Can you imagine how that small windowless room must have smelled, stuffed with rancid Etchemin?"

"Simply awful," Tamir volunteered, enjoying the egg hunt.

"And in the winter, that's when most of the Etchemin would die. But since the ground was frozen, the Etchemin would store the dead beneath the church, and wait for the land to thaw. Can you imagine what was worse, the smell of your unwashed neighbor praying beside you, or the smell of your dead friend rotting through the floorboards beneath you?"

"What a ghastly place the church must have been," Tamir replied, his hands filled with eggs. The boy had not found a single one, but they had enough.

"That is why the Etchemin would burn this vile plant, the one I marked on your head, young Annawon, to perfume away the stench of the dead and unclean, and clear your mind. Now come inside and let's eat, so I may give you your Hassun."

Tamir and the boy obeyed. The Algonquin cooked eggs and olives and spice, and the boy drank a bitter drink that burned his throat. The old woman told them many stories about the trees and the waters and the skies, for she was an Achak, an old spirit of the Algonquin, who had a message to deliver to them both.

"There is a reason you found me here on Skeleton Lake," she said as the forest grew dark. She explained how her people had grown up with the rocks and lakes, nomadics who traded furs and meats with the Huron, before the Iroquois came and killed the Algonquin, before the British came and killed the Iroquois, before Tamir and his father and others like them. Her tribe camped on the north shore, where the fish were plentiful and the deer would visit. But one winter the fish did not swim to that shore, and the deer did not visit. Her tribe moved camp, but one boy was not well and could not travel, so his Mother stayed with him so that he would not die alone. Settlers found two human skeletons on the north shore rocks, so the waters came to be called Skeleton Lake.

"If you do not follow The Way and journey to where life is abundant," she explained, "you too will die on the rocks of your own shore. And others close to you may die as well."

The boy found the old Indian woman intoxicating and strange.

"May I see the Hassun?" she asked the boy.

"I do not understand," the boy replied.

"Your stones. Have you not received them yet?" the woman asked, irritated. "No matter, they will arrive in time. I have one to give you, to keep with the others."

"What others?" the boy asked, confused.

The old woman sighed. "There is a bright light that shines around you, Annawon, which helps me see many things. You will receive stones, and these stones will be important. Do you know why?"

"No, I do not," the boy replied. He was not feeling well from the food and drink and was anxious to leave.

"The Professor will explain it to you," she said. "Here is mine to add." She handed the boy a small black rock. The boy took it, his hand shaking, for the old woman had mentioned the Professor by name. He wondered if the woman was a witch doctor who cast evil spells.

"Looks like a simple rock to me," Tamir said.

The old woman pointed at the boy. "And what do you see?" she demanded.

The boy could see his silhouette reflecting off the stone from the light of the fire. "I can see myself," he said.

"And so the rock is already at work on both of you!" the old woman cried out. "You are both correct. The Etchemin call this stone black tourmaline. But it is also called the rock of Capricorn, the one that protects against negative energy, lifts the spirits and grounds the first chakras and the corners of the earth." She clapped three times, then fell to the ground with a sudden crash, and her head drooped so severely that the two boys thought she had snapped her neck, but she eventually whispered.

"The dreams call us, yet when we hear the hawk's call we do not look to the sky. Do not be afraid, for the fear of failure is worse than the failure itself. Hold failure to your bosom like the old friend it will always be, for failure is what brings you closer to the energy of the universe. Every time you fail, you experience something new. You learn, you grow. Every time you try for something and do not get it, you understand more about the energy of that thing you desire. Failing always takes you forward, never backward. Failing connects you with the spirits, it connects you to the earth and rock. It connects you back with yourself."

The boy thought about this. "That doesn't make sense," he said. "If failure does all of that, what does success do?"

"Success blinds you," the Algonquin answered. "Unless you are able to adjust your eyes and see the true colors of success, not just its shadow and shape. If you channel the energy of the accomplishment, you can escape your cave and the sun will shine gladly upon you."

The old woman stood up, motioning that the meeting was over. The boys left quietly, and did not speak until they had past through the wet dark tunnel and back into the shimmering green waters of Skeleton Lake.

"You are like a brother to me," Tamir said eventually, "so I feel bad telling you this. You should not take the Algonquin words too seriously. My dad says the old woman is insane, that she has become crazy from living in the woods and talking to birds. He doesn't like me going to see her, but it is great fun."

"She knows about my dream, yet I told her nothing," the boy replied.

"My dad says that is a trick she uses," Tamir replied. "He says dreams are best left for artists, lovers and fools."

"Then why did you take me to see her?" the boy asked.

"I am not my father," Tamir said. "At least not yet."

That night the boy did not sleep. The Algonquin haunted him and he could envision her chanting and throwing burned plants. The odor was terrible, like the breath of an old dog, and he discovered he had not washed all the soot from his face, and the smell infected his pillow. When he finally fell asleep, he dreamed of the Algonquin and the Banker dancing together, first in a lavish ballroom and then on the shore of Skeleton Lake, and they were conversing.

"I own many things and I can live anywhere I chose," the Banker whispered.

"But can you live with the land and talk to wind?" the Algonquin whispered back.

"You must be happy being so rich," the Banker replied.

"I enjoy the process far more than the proceeds. How did you acquire your wealth?" she asked.

"I worked hard and believed in myself and did a few things right. And how did you acquire your wealth?"

"I followed my bliss," the Algonquin replied, then she turned into a cloud, leaving the Banker alone on the rocky shore.

The Muskoka summer days came and went. The boy woke early every morning and worked around the Banker's house, trimming grass, weeding flowers, painting docks and fixing equipment. The Banker paid him very well, and the boy made more money than he would have in the library, and he realized it was the happiest time of his life. The boy had decided that even though his certificate was worthless, it did not mean that he should give up trying to be like the Banker. He believed that his new path was The Way after all, and suddenly he realized that he had not dreamed about the dark girl all summer long. Not once did she arrive in the night, pointing at a page in a book. He missed the dream, but he was happy that she no longer came. He knew that the dark child was always with him, and he thanked the dream for sending him to the university where he met the Librarian and the Professor and especially Tamir, who had become like a brother and had introduced him to the Banker, who knew so much about being an Entrepreneur, and the Algonquin, who knew so much about the ways of the world.

✿

The boy completed his final year at the university with little difficulty. He was a good student, but he had chosen an unpopular profession, for war had come again and hard times had fallen across the land and there was little need for engineers. The boy wrote many letters requesting employment, but his offers were all promptly rejected. But the boy remained in high spirits, and kept the Algonquin's black rock by his bed. He started to once again write about his dreams, and when he was in dire straits and no offers for work arrived, he was thankful for his diary.

"Don't divorce yourself from your dreams," the Professor had said before. "When they are gone, you may still wander about, but you will no longer be alive." As he struggled to find work, the boy came to believe the Professor's words with all his heart.

As spring ensued prospective employers visited the university to meet with the students, but they did not call for the boy. The men who came to meet the students were not interested in engineers, but they were looking for bankers. So the boy did what he knew he should have done all along. He decided that he would no longer labor to be an engineer, as he had trained to do, but instead he would be a banker.

"Most unwise, to change your path," reported the official who served as counsel to the students. He was a short man with round glasses and a face so small that his head looked like a turtle peeking out from the shell of his collar. He was the Counselor, and it was his job to guide the graduating students down the proper career path, and help them find work once their studies were complete. The Counselor glanced at the boy's papers, pretending to look impressed and knowing.

"You should go where you can find work and be paid for your skills," the man explained. "The world does not pay for dreams. Once you leave this university, you cannot trust fantasy to put food on your table or a roof over your head. You must be realistic."

"But my dream is to become a banker and live in a large city," the boy said.

"You need to grow up and be a man, and let go of childish dreams," the Counselor insisted. "The world is a difficult place, and you cannot enter it ill-prepared. You must be pragmatic. You cannot be a banker, for you have not studied what bankers need to know. You must be an engineer, because that is what you have trained yourself to do. You cannot work in the big city, for engineers do not work in cities, they work in factories in the country."

"But I want to be a banker," the boy replied. "It is my dream."

"Son," the Counselor said, leaning close, "when we are young we dream, but as we grow and mature we understand that we must play our part in the machinery of the world. I had dreams when I was your age, dreams of playing music, but there was little money in it and I nearly starved. An ostrich does not dream of soaring in the skies, just as an eagle does not dream of running across the plains. Horses for courses, as we say. Listen to me, for I am wise and I have helped many students before you. You will face great difficulties once you leave this university, but if you understand that there are certain rules that are at work in the world, then you will do well enough."

"What rules do I need to know?" the boy asked.

"There are many, but the most important is the rule of focus. Focus brings clarity. That's the trouble with dreams; they are always out of focus. There is a reason for it. Focus means you train yourself in a certain skill, for a certain role, and then throw the weight of your heart and soul behind it. With a lot of hard work and a little luck, opportunities will present themselves, so long as you have the discipline to stay the course."

"But what course?" the boy replied.

"That is simple," the Counselor replied. "It is the course you have already chosen for yourself. This university offers so many different paths, and you have chosen to be an engineer. Focus your energy there. That is The Way you should go."

The boy knew that in fact he did not choose to be an engineer, that it had been chosen for him by the teachers, because the classes he wanted to take were all filled, because his Father refused to drive him to the university in time.

"It's my Father's fault," the boy replied. "It was the only way available to me when I arrived here."

The Counselor laughed, waving him off. "If I had a coin for every time I heard an excuse from a student, I would be a king. Let me give you some advice. You cannot go through life blaming others, like your parents or your teachers or your world. Take responsibility for your own decisions and actions, and only then will you be successful in your quest. You are an engineer; that was your decision and yours alone. Now you need to decide if you want to be the best engineer you can be."

The boy left the Counselor's office nodding, but inside he knew he would not be an engineer. He wanted to be a banker and work in the city. His dream was leading him there, and he was compelled to follow it.

"I will be the best banker ever," the boy said, and he felt strange hearing himself say it out loud.

Summer approached and the students at the university were offered employment in their desired fields. But not the boy. Though he wrote many letters and sent his papers to all the banks, he received no interest. As the last days of the university session drew near, there was a grand ceremony, but the boy was too embarrassed to attend, and watched from the bench by the chapel as the happy students left with their families and their boxes and their new opportunities.

"I shall take the bus home tomorrow to live with Mother and work for Father," the boy sighed. "Father will rejoice, for he predicted my fate, and said I would discover that his world is the best world of all. But in my heart I do not believe it." The boy was deep in thought, considering his fate, when a man sat down on the bench next to him.

"Is the student ready?" the man asked. The boy looked up. It was the Professor, dressed in blue regalia with a square cap and long, flowing gown.

"I am a graduate of this university, Professor," the boy replied, trying to sound chipper. "My education is complete."

"Education is mainly about what you unlearn," the Professor replied, sitting down next to the boy. "Have your studies here been nothing but a sleepy taqleed? Have you not unlearned anything?"

The boy thought for a moment. "I don't know about that, but I know that one day I will be a great success as a banker."

"Good for you!" the Professor smiled. "All you need is confidence and ignorance and your success is guaranteed."

The boy looked at the Professor, confused.

"Yes, I suppose that's not very encouraging given your situation," the Professor confessed. "Anyway, all generalizations are false, including that one. So tell me, did you find The Way?"

The boy did not answer, for he had long forgotten what the Professor had said about The Way.

The Professor looked discouraged. "Then I will remind you. You once told me of a beautiful dream about a child who comes to you, hands you a book, and points to a page marked with a signpost to your treasure, your wealth and eternal happiness."

"An allegory," the boy replied, sounding fastidious. "That is correct."

"More than an allegory...a map! Why do you refuse this map? Very few in this world are handed the map that shows them The Way, yet you disposed of yours!"

The boy stood up to leave.

"I was afraid of that," the Professor continued, "which is why I have something for you. Seems you need it." He reached into his gown and pulled out a small red satchel, tied closed with twine.

"What is that?" the boy asked, sitting back down.

"Depends on who's looking, and what they want to see," the Professor replied. "To most people, it's simply a bag of rocks. But to some, they are much more than rocks. Reach in and take one."

The boy remembered what the Algonquin had said, and became concerned that the old woman had placed a spell over him. He was educated to put faith in the physical and methodical ways of the world and was steeped in equations and analytics, so much so that he was barren and closed to forces such as fortune telling and mystic energy. But yet the Algonquin's words now rang true.

The boy reached into the Professor's satchel and retrieved a smooth, rounded pebble. It was milky white, with veins of green coursing throughout.

"That's a good one for you," the Professor smiled with approval. "Now tell me what you see."

"It is moss agate," the boy replied confidently, happy for once to have studied engineering. "The white substance is quartz, and the green filaments are an oxide of iron and manganese."

"That is how the Scientist would define it," the Professor replied. "Tell me what you see, not what it is."

"Is this some sort of trick?' the boy asked.

"No, and yes. What do you see?"

The boy inspected the stone carefully.

"This pattern of green embedded in the white looks like a network of paths, connecting in every which way," the boy said, "like what roads might look like if you were a bird flying high in the sky. It is a map of sorts, that goes round and round."

"I am impressed," the Professor said. "You saw with your mind, not your eyes. Your eyes will deceive you, so do not trust them. Trust your mind, and you will have the vision you need for The Way."

"What is so special about moss agate?" the boy asked.

"Absolutely nothing at all," the Professor replied. "The Indians thought it brought truth and spiritual guidance. They believed those filaments represented a powerful plant living inside the cold stone. Life within death, movement inside stillness. The real question is: what is so special about this stone that compelled you to choose it now?"

"I do not know. It felt smooth and polished, and perhaps I grabbed it because I don't feel so smooth and polished myself."

"Now you are learning!" the Professor exclaimed, pleased. "You recognize that you need to continue your search and further develop your self-identity, for which you still need a map. Bravo, boy!"

"It seems so silly," the boy declared.

"Only if you believe in silly things. If you believe in important things, then the significance of that stone is very important." The man tied the twine and handed the red satchel to the boy. "This is yours. Keep it with you at all times, but never look inside of it, for the stones will present themselves when you are ready."

"When will I be ready?" the boy asked.

"When you come to a fork in your path," the Professor said, "when The Way becomes difficult to see, pull a stone from the satchel and allow it to guide you. But use them wisely, for the power comes from within you, not from within this pouch. Can you remember that?"

"I will," the boy replied.

"Good luck on your journey," the Professor said, and he stood up, wiped off his smock and whistled like a bluebird as he made his way across the bluegrass lawn. This time he did not spin around on his heels and shout.

Later that day, Tamir found the boy sitting on the bench, deep in thought.

"I told my dad about your search," Tamir said, "and he agreed to help."

"You didn't need to do that," the boy replied.

"It was no trouble at all," Tamir replied. "Unfortunately his business is slowing, and he is letting go of good people, so he cannot hire you. But he gave me the number of a man at a bank in Baghdad who might be able to help."

The boy stared at the paper Tamir handed to him and smiled, for there was a telephone number scrawled on the page, and it contained a ten and a thirteen, just like the numbers on the page in his dream.

"I don't know how to thank you," the boy said.

"I am the one who must thank you," Tamir replied. "You have been like a brother to me these past years. I came to this university frightened and lifeless, dumber than a scarecrow. But you helped me see how smart I really was. You showed me The Way."

"I didn't do anything," the boy replied.

"That's the beauty of it," Tamir said. "For you it was effortless. For me it meant everything. When you find your treasure in Baghdad some day, I hope you will remember me."

"I will always," the boy replied. They shook hands and embraced, then Tamir left the boy alone on the bench, and the boy was sad that he would not see his friend ever again.

✿

PART THREE

The number on the page connected the boy to a woman who transferred him to a man who directed him to another person at a bank who told the boy he needed to be in Baghdad in three days and not a day later.

"It does not pay much but it is a foot in the door," the boy considered. "It is simply hasan, nothing more than permissible employ."

The job was not important. It entailed stuffing envelopes and delivering booklets, but the boy was very grateful. He thought about the Counselor and was glad he did not follow his advice. He considered himself lucky to have found any job at all, since the great depression was not ending, and war was erupting all around the country. The next day he sold all that he could of his belongings and purchased a bus ticket south to Baghdad, with a connection through Samarra. He had never been to Samarra and wanted to see the ancient mud brick sites and the Matwiya Tower and the shrine of Muhammed al-Mahdi before continuing on to Baghdad.

The bus arrived at the university before dawn, as the dark night sky melted into azure. The bus was silver and cobalt and covered in dust, with dirty blue cushions, and though the boy was tired and the seats invited him to sleep, he did not want to miss anything that passed by the windows. He did not talk to the other passengers, and the others did not talk to him, for each was on a journey of their own.

The boy thought about the old men and women at the nursing home, and guessed at who might have already died and who might still be alive. He wondered if he might spend his last days with the Nurse, and then wondered if his Mother would go there soon, and this made him sad so he stopped thinking about home.

He thought about the students he had met at the university and wished them all well on their adventures, but he worried about not heeding the Counselor's advice, which still haunted him. So he thought about the Professor, and took the red satchel out of his rucksack and caressed it.

"One day when it is time I will withdraw a stone, but not today, for today I am on the right path," he said to himself. He decided that any doubts he had would vanish as soon as he arrived in Baghdad. It was the happiest he had been since his summer with Tamir in Muskoka.

The sun was bright when he stepped into the station at Samarra. A cacophony of shouting vendors and bustling commuters erupted on the platform, but to the boy it was a strange, seductive music calling out to him. He checked the time of the last bus heading north, then set out on foot to explore the city.

The boy walked to the Tell Sawwan and the Malwiya Tower and to the ruins of the Al Askariya mosque and basked in the glow of the history and destruction and rebirth of all the monuments and buildings. He marveled at how many birds populated the city, perched it seemed on every building and statue. Since he had little money, he did not buy food or souvenirs, but he threw three coins in a shrine fountain and made a wish. Towards the end of the day his hunger overcame him, and he purchased two golden apples from a street cart and devoured them beside the teal waters of the Tigris. They were in his opinion the best apples he had ever eaten.

He crossed the Tigris via a long bridge and entered an endless cemetery, where the bodies of thousands of men and women were lined cap to boot beneath the rolling turquoise hills. The tombs of the soldiers and the memorials to war pulled a somber weight down on the boy. He was respectful of the death and honor sleeping beneath the ground, but he could not pray. As the wind increased, bringing cool air from distant oceans, the boy stood at a large tomb, caressing the hard cerulean stone. His Father was not a soldier, but the boy fancied that if the Great War called him that he would be a strong and valiant hero.

"Fighting is nothing to be proud of," a voice said below. The boy turned and faced a man sitting in a wheelchair. He wore a navy jacket covered with patches and ribbons and a large sapphire medal with the image of a white dove inside. He was a Soldier.

"I am not called to jihad," the boy replied.

"Perhaps you are called to Jahiliyyah," the crippled Soldier replied.

"I am going to be a banker."

"Nobody ever wants to fight. But anyone who believes in something will eventually have to fight for it."

"There is war surrounding me, but I am far away from it, and I will not be called into it," the boy replied.

The Soldier shrugged, pushed his arms with a grunt and rolled his wheelchair down the path. At the cemetery gates he stopped and spun around.

"The fighting is closer than you know," the Soldier warned, then disappeared.

The sky was darker than it should have been, and the air colder. The boy studied the horizon and saw that a great mass of black clouds had converged over Samarra. As he ran across the long bridge back towards the station, a summer thunderstorm erupted and the birds disappeared and the people ran underground and water flooded the streets. In the storm the boy could not find his way. A clock bell chimed in the distance and the boy realized his bus was about to depart, but in the rain and darkness he was lost.

It was still raining when he reached the station, but the station was no longer crowded with people scurrying about like bees in a concrete hive. He found the last dispatcher who informed him that the southern line had departed, and that he would have to wait until the morning for the next bus for Baghdad.

"What a fool I am," the boy said to himself. He found a bench in the back of the station and hid, for he intended to stay the night on the platform, for he knew that if he missed the morning bus he would lose his job at the bank. "It was unwise of me to wander about and enjoy myself so, when I should have been patient and waited here in the station for my bus. It serves me right for straying off my path." The boy was very mad at himself, and he crossed his arms and scowled at the floor.

He did not notice the three men approaching on padded feet.

"What are you doing in our station?" one of the men barked.

The boy looked up. The men were standing above him, snarling, wrapped in thick coats so that they appeared much larger, as dogs do when they raise their fur.

"I am waiting for my bus," the boy replied, looking away.

"Give us your money," another man growled. He moved closer to the boy, and the boy could smell his breath, which was worse than the soot the Algonquin had smeared on his forehead.

"I am afraid I have no money to give," the boy replied, his voice laced with terror.

"Hand over your sack, and you may live," the third man snapped. The men shuffled closer, and the boy could see nothing but an enormous mass of coats and legs and fur supporting three heads, each grinning at him with wet yellow teeth.

The boy gathered his courage and jumped to his feet. He was a strong boy, and as he stood he saw concern flash in the men's eyes, but they did not retreat. One man reached for his rucksack and the boy pushed him away, preparing for a fight. Everything he owned in the world was in his sack, and he was not going to depart with it so easily.

"What's going on over there?" a voice erupted from across the platform, and an official-looking man came running towards them.

"Lucky for you," one of the heads snarled. "But no matter. We'll be waiting for you outside. You can't stay here tonight, and you'll have to pass us. Then you'll pay with your life." The men pushed the boy to the ground and trotted away.

"Are you hurt?" the man in a red jacket asked, extending his hand. The boy knew not to talk to strangers, but the man was formally dressed in a smart jacket that read 'Ferryman Deliveries' in large letters. "My name is Charon," the man reassured. "I am a driver. Did they rob you?"

"No, I am fine," the boy replied, clutching his rucksack.

"Cities are dangerous places. This station is not safe at such a late hour. Where are you from, and where are you heading?"

"I'm from the northern country," the boy replied, brushing himself off. "I am going to Baghdad, but I missed my bus."

"Beautiful city," Charon smiled with a wide grin, and the boy saw that the man had many teeth capped in silver, reflecting the light as if an obol was tucked in his mouth. "First time in Samarra, I assume. Well, the bad news is all the southern lines have left for tonight. The next bus bound for Baghdad is not until tomorrow morning, and you can't stay here."

"I have no choice," the boy acknowledged.

"You always have choices," the man said, still smiling. "But there is good news. I am here at this hour to collect a package and drive it to Baghdad. For a small fee, I could take you south."

"When?" the boy asked.

"I am leaving now," the man replied. "As I said, I am a driver and I have my own truck. It's not fancy, but it will get you across the river and down the line better than any. People are like packages, always needing to be delivered."

The boy could not believe his luck. "I don't have much money to pay you," the boy confessed.

"How much do you have?" Charon asked.

The boy reached into his pocket and waved his neatly folded money.

"Put that back in your pocket, son!" the man demanded. "You don't want to attract more attention. You can ride in my truck. Come; let's leave before those men come back."

The boy was delighted. He would get to Baghdad tonight after all. He was happy he did not have to wait until morning for the bus or face the three robbers again.

"The universe conspires to aid you in every step," he thought, and as he followed Charon, the boy could not believe his good fortune. "Everything happens for a reason," he said out loud, and he believed it.

The man in the red jacket scurried down some stairs and outside to where many trucks were parked. The rain was heavy but the boy did not mind. Charon ducked behind a large red truck, and when the boy caught up with him, he could see that the man was holding something in his hands.

"What is that?" the boy asked.

"Sticks," Charon replied, spinning about. He jumped and swung a metal chain and two heavy sticks crushed the boy's face. The boy fell back onto the ground, blood pouring out of his eyes.

"Give me your money and your things," the man hissed.

"I thought you were driving me to Baghdad!" the boy cried out. The earth spun in circles and the boy could not see.

"I warned you that this is a dangerous place," Charon spat. "You don't have enough money for the journey. So you will give it all to me, in exchange for your life."

"No, I beg of you!" the boy pleaded. "It is all I have!"

"Tell it to your gods," Charon demanded, and he hit the boy many times with his sticks, until the boy could not move. As the man dug through the sack, the boy hugged the wet ground, for he was blind and felt as if he were falling off the earth.

"What's this?" the man yelled out. "A bag of rocks? What a fool you are, carrying rocks." He threw the bag at the boy, hitting him in the mouth. "You are so stupid. I feel sorry for you; you are so easy to steal from. You should not trust people so much. The world is an evil place. Some people never learn that, and this is what happens to them." The man howled with laughter and disappeared.

The boy could not give chase. Blinded by the dark bâtil, the pain infected his mind and he curled up on the wet ground, bleeding, blind and cold. His breathing slowed and his eyes welled shut, and the sound of the rain extinguished all other sounds around him, and eventually the sound of the rain extinguished, and the boy floated off to a quiet, black space.

A mosque bell rang in the distance, and then the boy heard the sound of trains. He felt the ground warming and remembered how glorious that morning had been, waking up before dawn, walking to the university bus station and setting off on his journey. He thought about all the farms and fields and towns he saw as the bus made its way south to Samarra. He thought about walking in the warm sun and seeing the great monuments and the cemetery and the wounded Soldier, and eating apples in the shadow of the great golden dome. What a wonderful day it had been.

And now he was beaten, robbed and blind, pushed into the womb of munkar, alone in a strange, dangerous city, with no money and no way back home. His dream had become a nightmare, all in the course of a single day.

"How quickly fortunes can turn. I wish I had stayed home with Mother," he said out loud, and hearing his own voice awakened him, and he opened his eyes. His vision was blurred and he could see only shadows. He was frightened, he was angry and he was ashamed, and since he was all alone, he cried in self-pity and despair. It was the first time he had cried since his Father had left.

The boy looked up at the station clock. It was morning. He had missed his bus to Baghdad, but it didn't matter, for he had no money.

He heard people approaching, whispering.

"Look, Cephas, he is alive," a woman said.

"He that sleeps in the mud of the earth shall awake to everlasting life, or maybe to shame and everlasting contempt," another woman said.

"Oh, stop your rambling!" another voice scolded.

The boy stirred as a man grabbed his arms and three women grabbed his feet. They carried him across the parking lot and laid him next to a shopping cart filled with bags and blankets.

"Qabîluhu!" the boy cried, trying to wave them away.

"Fear not, dear nafs. We thought you were dead, but we didn't want to tell the authorities or the elders," the man said. He smiled and the boy saw that some of his teeth were missing and that he had not bathed in a long time. "You've been lying there for three days. You're lucky the weather's been so bad; otherwise they would have hauled you away. Here, take this, you need it more than we do." The man handed the boy an apple and a can filled with water.

"Thank you," the boy muttered. He ate the apple, core and all. The man and the three women helped him up, then left him alone, so that he could consider his fate.

"Three days! Damn you, stupid dream!" the boy shouted, lifting his hardened face. The rain had ended but clouds still held the sky. He had no money, no clean clothes, and even if he did find a way to Baghdad there would be no work waiting for him. He shook his fist into the air. "I was content just to live my life as it was laid out for me! I was happy helping the old people. They looked forward to seeing me in the morning and I comforted them at night. They trusted me, and I trusted them. But now I have followed a childish dream, and that dream has stripped from me all that I have, all of my money and four years of my life. The driver was right, I am stupid to trust others, and I am stupid to believe in myself!"

He thought of his Mother, alone in her apartment, wishing about her distant son who had promised to return home with great wealth. She had given him everything she could give, and the boy had wasted it all.

He thought of his Father and realized that his Father was right, and it hurt the boy deeply to admit it.

Lightening flashed and morning thunder rolled above the city, and the boy knew it to be an omen, that the world was laughing at his misfortune. As he stood and stewed in his shame and misfortune, a strange feeling grew inside of him, for the thought of the universe laughing at him angered the boy, and slowly he mustered up a steely resolve.

"I will fight you," the boy cried out. "I will not quit!" He shook his fist, and the heavens opened up and the rain began again.

He found his rucksack, torn and crumpled in the mud and gravel. The man had taken everything except his diary. Beside it was the red satchel the Professor had given him, still filled with stones. With a sigh of relief the boy shook the purse and tried to pray.

"If there ever was a time I needed guidance, this is it," he said as he pulled out a stone. It was white, with pink ribbons running through it, smooth and round as if it had come from the bottom of a river, plain and dull as a rock could be. He held it in his hands and inspected it for a long time, wondering what omen it brought, but all he could see was an ordinary stone; no signpost or signal presented itself for his review.

"I am to blame, not my dream," he said at last, for he realized blaming his dream was no different than blaming himself. "My dream is me, we are one and the same. I cannot blame God or the universe or anyone else for my misfortune. My life is my responsibility, and I must accept it fully." And as the boy sat in the rain and wondered what he should do, he was no longer frightened, for he had nothing left to steal but a bag of rocks, his diary and his dreams.

"Where is The Way leading me?" he asked the stone as if it were a ball of crystal like the ones the gypsies used. "Do I go home and start again? Do I start from here and press on? Or do I take a new direction entirely?" He held the white stone tight in his hands, and the numbness in his arms melted away, and the boy felt warm. The rain slowed and then stopped, but the boy did not move, and watched in silent mediation as the clouds sailed off, allowing a honey light to paint the horizon. As the sun warmed the earth, the boy could see he had been lying in the corner of a parking lot.

"That is the sign," he said at last, gazing across the lot filled with trucks and abandoned equipment, and he began to laugh, for the ground was covered with stones, stones of the same shape and color as the one he had pulled out of the Professor's pouch.

"A piece of gravel," the boy laughed, and suddenly his heart was filled with relief. He had been robbed, beaten and left for dead on the cold wet earth for three days; he had not a coin to his name, but yet he still had purpose, and that was all that he needed.

"I will stay here, for the stone says this is where I am supposed to be at this time. I will work here until I earn enough to get safely to Baghdad, to continue my journey," he said, and his own confidence surprised him. "Every step may not take me forward, but every step is a step in my journey, and I will follow The Way wherever it may take me. And when I do find my wealth in Baghdad, it will taste that much sweeter."

The boy stood up, wiped off his face and hands and clothes as best he could, kissed the white stone, and walked into the new sun rising.

☼

Work was difficult to find. The boy was too proud to beg, too good to steal and too ashamed to call his Mother. His clothes were soiled and his face was infected and scarred, so even kind people were afraid of him and waved him away. They judged the boy as he judged his diary book: torn, dirty and purposeless. But still the boy pushed on, walking south, in the direction of the industrial cities. He was able to find small errands along the way which paid for food, and he was offered fruit and nuts and drink by Samaritans who passed him and felt sorry for his situation. He slept in the streets at night and looked for work in the day, and his face grew tough like leather and his eyes grew distant and wandering.

One evening he found shelter in an abandoned shed in the shadow of a factory outside of Samarra. The next morning he was awoken by a noisy caravan of brown cars that parked nearby. The boy hid and watched as three smartly dressed men spilled out of the cars and approached the factory.

"He does not keep his facility very tidy," a man wearing gold glasses remarked.

"I agree," said another man. "Frankly I sense that this manager will not impress, for a man who cannot keep his yard in order cannot be trusted to tend to his shop."

"Yes, it would give me more encouragement if he cared for all aspects of his kingdom," the third man said.

The factory door opened and the three men entered. The boy thought they were wise and their comments astute. He studied his own clothes and hands and realized why he had so much trouble finding work, for his outside appearance was pitiful. He searched for some water and washed himself completely, and while he was drying himself in the sun the factory door opened and the three men left in their cars.

When he was ready, the boy knocked on the factory door and a large, round man answered.

"As sala'amu alaikum, sir. I am here to work," the boy announced.

"Bismillah! I did not ask for any help," the man replied, looking around with concern. "Go away at once, or I shall call the police."

"Sir, you need my help," the boy insisted. "I bring a message from the three men who just visited here."

The round man looked down upon the boy with suspicion. "Boy, I am the Manager of this factory, and I have already received my message from them."

"Not the one I bring," the boy replied.

The Manager looked down at the boy with curiosity and wondered what to make of this visit. "You are the second meeting I have had this morning, the second interruption unplanned," the Manager said. "I do not believe in coincidence, so I will play your game. Tell me, what message do you bring from my largest customer?"

"Largest customer today, but not tomorrow," the boy replied. "For they worry about this place."

"You are wrong, gypsy boy. They are coming back next week, and they will place a handsome order," the Manager replied.

"Are you certain? They are not impressed with how the outside of your factory appears," the boy reported. "It is said that a man who cannot take care of his yard has trouble taking care of his customers. If those men are important to you, then their words should be important as well."

The Manager nodded his head in agreement. "It is strange that you should arrive here at this time," he said, "for I was just thinking about cleaning up my yard. But I have workers who can do such things. Why should I pay you to do it?"

"Three reasons, sir," the boy replied. "I am the first to warn you, so you should honor that. Second, even though you have workers who can clean your yard, none of them have stepped forward, so I doubt they would work with as much passion and care as I would. And third, I need to earn money so that I may eat, and eventually get to Baghdad, to become a banker."

The Manager threw back his head and laughed so hard that his whole face turned violet, and the boy wondered if he was in great pain. "I am sorry, gypsy boy," he chuckled. "You would need to clean my yard for an entire year to earn enough money to get to Baghdad!"

"If that is what it takes," the boy insisted, "I will gladly do it."

The Manager rubbed his fat chin and studied the boy. "Insha'allah…you have great spirit, but I don't need your services. You should go home and ask your parents for money, but not me, for I am not a charity. I run a factory, and these are difficult times, and I have my own children to feed."

"My parents do not have any money," the boy confessed. His heart sank as his dream drifted further away. He thought about the lights of the city, the busy people, the bankers in their buildings and the energy in the streets. His mind fell into darkness, and that darkness reflected in his eyes. The boy stood in silence, fighting back tears that welled inside of him. The Manager watched him, intrigued with how tenacious and persistent the boy was, much more so, he thought, than many of the people who worked inside his factory.

"I will clean your yard," the boy said at last, straightening his spine and looking the Manager square in the eye. "If you like my work, you can pay me whatever you want. If you don't approve of my work, then you pay me nothing. You don't have to pay me either way. But I sense you are a good man, and you take care of your customers and your workers and your family, and so I will trust you."

"I am a stranger to you. Why trust me?" the Manager asked. "What if you work hard and I refuse to pay you?"

"Trusting in others is one of the few things I have left, and nobody can take that from me," the boy said.

The Manager thought about his important customer, and he saw how dirty the yard was. He thought about his accountant who was always spilling food on himself, which worried him, for he believed that a man who could not bring a fork correctly to his mouth could not be trusted to manage his financial affairs.

"There is a reason you are here, today, on the day my biggest customer surprises me with a visit," the Manager said. "Your dress certainly does not rise to the level of your passion, so listen close. Move all the crates and boxes to the back. There is a trailer in the stockyard with a cot where you can sleep for a few days. I will give you food, not as an advance against your payment, but because I am a religious man, and I believe in the story of the Good Samaritan."

"If I do a good job, will you hire me to work in your factory?" the boy asked.

"Times are tough, gypsy," the Manager said. "When I return in a few days, we will discuss it, after I inspect your work."

"Thank you, sir," the boy said, bowing. "You are a kind man."

"Maybe I am not. You should judge me when I return, for that is when I shall judge you." The Manager showed the boy the trailer and brought him some bread and raisins, and wished him well.

Tiny flakes puffed out of the smokestacks all day. The violet ash fell like snow upon the weedy yard and warm asphalt, invisible to all except the boy. He repaired the splintered crates and hauled away debris and stacked rows of kindling, but he could not exterminate the purple soot that penetrated the stone and concrete of the yards. The boy swept it up into volcanic piles and scooped it into bags, never to be inhaled again, but every day the factory would belch more. The boy coughed and bled and strained for five days, and the pollution from the factory burned him, but his will burned hotter.

When the Manager returned he was happy. The factory yard was cleaner and better organized than it had been in many years. When the three men appeared again in their brown cars they all remarked on the improvements and assumed that business was doing well, and they placed a larger order than the Manager had expected.

The Manager saw the boy's arrival as a good omen and invited him into his office. The boy had never been inside of the factory, and as he followed the round man up the stairs, he gazed upon all the people at work below.

"You were right to judge my yard's appearance, and I am glad I was wrong judging yours," the Manager said, and he paid the boy a fair wage. "You are welcome to stay longer and do more cleaning, for the inside of the factory is as bad as the outside once was, and your work will be appreciated by all. Times are difficult and I cannot pay you much, but you may live in my trailer for a while."

"I am very grateful," the boy replied, "but I will stay only until I have enough money to get to Baghdad, so that I can become the banker I dream of becoming."

"Very well. Come, I will introduce you to the workers, and they will show you what needs to be done." As they were leaving the office, the boy studied the factory floor and all its equipment and people and boxes.

"Tell me, sir," the boy asked, "What do you make here?"

"This is a bindery," the Manager replied. "We make books, books that people use for writing notes and keeping diaries."

☼

The boy worked hard in the factory. He cleaned the walls, the floors and windows inside and out, he cleaned all the equipment, including the pre-press stations, the film processors, the plate burners and stripping tables, the offset printers and the conveyers and the bindery, including the saddle-stitch machines and the folders and the laminating machines and the die cutters. All the workers liked the boy, for he posed no threat to their jobs and he always helped them, no matter what was needed.

When customers came to visit the factory they always commented on how clean the floors were and how shiny the equipment was, and they placed many orders for books, and this made the Manager very pleased, so pleased that he increased the boy's wage, and the boy was able to buy new clothes. He still lived in the trailer, for he did not want to spend his money on an apartment.

As he worked and earned a small wage, the boy became aware of the real world and gradually let go of his dream of going to Baghdad to be a banker. He grew much more pragmatic, realistic and mature, as the Counselor had said he would. He no longer wrote in his diary, for now he was surrounded by stacks and stacks of blank books, and he knew what was written in every single one, and he accepted that he was living his dream, and he was happy.

One day he counted the money he had saved and saw that he had enough to buy a bus ticket, but he did not want to leave immediately, for he was earning a fair wage and he had made friends among the workers. Everyone in the factory depended upon him, especially the jolly Manager, for over time the boy did more than just sweep floors and clean machines. He fixed the equipment, he made improvements on the factory line, he adjusted settings and he developed new ways to make the bindings, things that nobody had ever thought of, and each of these changes made the customers happy and they ordered more and more books.

"These are difficult times, and in difficult times people need our books to scribble down their dreams," the Manager would often say, and then add: "But the boy is the secret to our new success."

That day when he counted his money and realized he had earned enough to go back home, he caressed the white gravel stone that he kept above his cot and he cried. His job paid well but it would never amount to great wealth, and he was quite happy in the book factory, for he knew he was following his dream, the dream that the dark child had showed to him. But he knew he would have to return home, because like most boys his age, he was restless and hungry for companionship.

At the end of each week the workers would visit a nearby tavern for wine and song. The boy never took part, for he was occupied with saving his money, but when the workers came to understand his plight, they carried him to the tavern to buy him wine and tell him stories. There the boy learned he was not the only one chasing a dream. Some of the workers were younger than the boy, and they shared their visions of the future and what they hoped to do with the rest of their lives, but the older workers had given up on their dreams, and were content to labor their lives away in the book factory.

One evening at the tavern the boy was offered purple wine and he became confused and lost in his own thoughts, so he sat at a table alone. Eventually a man with a large flat chest and silver hair sat next to him. The boy recognized him from the factory; he worked in the bindery and was in charge of keeping all the equipment well-oiled and running smoothly. His name was Rafig, but everyone called him the Mechanic, because he would walk up and down the bindery conveyer belt, holding his cutter like an ax, checking the gears and tin press sheets. He marched along as if he had steel pins in his legs, and the other workers said that he had been in the Great War and still had metal throughout his body, and that he took to bindery maintenance because it was similar to working on tanks.

"Fetch me an oil can," the Mechanic creaked at the tavern owner, "and a can of that oil you call beer for the boy." When the beer arrived the old man drank his down in one gulp, then shouted, "Empty as a kettle!"

The boy was not feeling well and wanted to simply click his heals and be home. The old man frightened him, for he was certainly drunk. The other workers said he loved to drink, and he loved to eat honey, and that he ate so much of it that bees were rumored to settle on his lips.

The old man leaned back and pounded his chest. "All hollow in here, you see? No heart. What about you, boy? Are you still tender and gentle and friendly with sparrows?"

The boy nodded. He sipped the beer, thinking the old man was right, it did taste like oil.

"Do you think the factory boss is helping you?" the Mechanic asked. "Or is he hurting you?" The boy looked over and could see that the man's platus was as wide as the Tigris River, and he could not keep from staring at it.

"He is full of tayyib…of course he is helping me," the boy finally said. "He has given me a place to live, and he pays me for my work."

The old man's face was stiff. "Sorry to rain on your parade, but who benefits most from such an arrangement?" the Mechanic asked.

"And well he should, since he is an Entrepreneur, and I am but a Journeyman," the boy replied.

"Why do you believe there is any difference between being an Entrepreneur and being a Journeyman?"

"It would not matter much to me either way, for one day I will be wealthy and I will live in a big city and find a wife and make lots of money," the boy replied, confident, though the wine made his voice sluggish.

"It is good that you have heart, and that you believe in dreams," the Mechanic shrugged. "It takes great practice to interpret one's dreams. I used to have dreams too, but they were difficult to read, and I didn't have my heart in it. I spent much of my younger days chasing things when I should have sat back and waited for them to come to me. The Way is like that. Do you know The Way?"

The boy thought about the Professor. "I have heard about it," he replied. "I believe that if you discover The Way, you should focus all your energies on it and follow it to the end of time."

"So, have you found The Way?"

"I think so," the boy said, but he wasn't sure.

"Then you have not," the Mechanic replied, sensing doubt in the boy's voice. "For if you knew The Way, you would be absolutely sure of yourself. Since you are not sure of yourself, how can you be happy? And if you are unhappy, you have not found The Way. Now, here is the great secret. It is easy to find The Way. If you are troubled by something, take action. Think only good thoughts, think only about what you want and what makes you happy, and like a magic curtain lifted, The Way reveals itself to you. It amazes me that the young people today are not told this. What did they teach you at the university?"

The boy never mentioned to the Manager or any of the workers that he had come from the university, out of shame for his predicament, and wondered how the Mechanic had known this.

"I learned many things," the boy confessed. "I have learned of the power of sadaqa."

"Did you learn the difference between knowledge and belief?"

"Certainly," the boy replied with some confidence. "Knowledge is understanding the things of the world, and belief is understanding why the things of the world are what they are."

The old man crinkled his wide forehead. "You didn't learn anything. If you know something it is an eternal truth, it never changes. A belief is a contingent truth. That is the great dualism, isn't it? There's the real world, all the stuff we see and taste, like this oily beer, and the perceptual world, like energy and ideas and beliefs. You have to use your intellect to perceive them both. The question is, do you truly know what you believe?"

The old man stood up and pounded the table with an iron fist.

"Do you not recognize me? Do you not see your Wali? I had a dream once, when I was your age. I wanted to travel to the deepest forests, in the north, find some land and fell some trees and build a house and raise a family. But I went to war and my dream ended. So I came here to make books, so that I still might cut and shape the trees. But it is the great lie, this rationalization, because I have no heart in it. The secret is, when you are following your dream and you know it with all your heart, the entire world conspires to help you."

The Mechanic put his hand on the boy's shoulder and smiled.

"Your arrival has been a blessing for all of us at the factory, especially me," he said, and the boy was touched, even though he knew the man was drunk. "I have watched you; you have such heart in everything you do, and those of us who have lost our way have seen the hope in your eyes. You have given us all heart again, and for that, we all thank you."

With a stiff limp the old man marched out the door, and the boy noticed that the tavern was empty, and he was alone.

The boy finished his beer, but he did not enjoy it. It was late and his head was spinning. He wanted to go back to the factory yard and climb onto his cot and dream about the dark girl pointing to the page where his treasure waited, for now he missed her very much, and wanted only to dream and dream.

✿

It was winter when the Manager called the boy into his office a second time.

"You have made my factory beautiful and my customers happy," the Manager said. "You were right about cleaning the yard, and you were right about improving the book stitching and the wooden covers and the pallet stacks. You have good ideas and I have accepted many of them."

"Thank you, sir," the boy replied, polite as always.

"But these are difficult times, so I want you to spend more time with the customers, and develop new books to sell them, since you seem to be able to anticipate their needs."

"Your customers are like my patients in the hospital at home," the boy replied. "You just need to listen to them with some care."

"I will pay you a commission for any new customers you bring to me, the same that I give everyone else." Though the Manager believed that the boy was indeed a gypsy, he also believed in omens, so he offered the boy what he offered his other workers.

"But before you spend time with the important customers," he continued, "you need to understand how the business of making books really works."

"I am ready now, sir," the boy replied. "I can work every machine in the factory. I know everything there is to know about pre-press and paper stock and cutting and binding and gluing and wrapping and shipping."

"Yet you have so much more to learn," the Manager said. "You may know how to run the machines, but you do not know how to run a business. If you want to be an Entrepreneur one day you must know things you cannot see, things which aren't run by a machine, such as setting prices and managing customers and counting receipts and debating contracts."

"I want to learn these things," the boy admitted, and it was true.

"I thought you might," the Manager replied, "so you will start in the ledgers and check the figures, for that is the best place to learn about a business." He led the boy to the back of the factory and up a rickety staircase and into a dark room, where a small wooden desk sat, surrounded by stacks and stacks of thick books.

"These ledgers hold all my financial records," the Manager said. "Those papers on the desk contain all of the orders from this year. I want you to check them and see if any customers have forgotten to pay us."

A week later the boy showed the Manager what he had found and the Manager was very impressed, for the boy had discovered many errors in the accounting records, and suggested ways to improve the financial affairs of the factory. On the spot, the Manager doubled the boy's wage and gave him responsibility for managing the accounting books for the entire factory.

"I will be able to go home very soon," the boy later calculated. "I will arrive in a new suit and shower my Mother with gifts." He determined that if he stayed until the following spring, he could earn enough to buy a television for the hospital.

"I have the dream to thank," the boy said to himself. "If I had not followed my dream, I would not have found a way to make such a high wage. The journey has been difficult, and there were times when I wanted to quit. But I was strong and I keep pushing myself. Now here I am, in a factory filled with books, outside of a big city, earning lots of money, just as the dream depicted."

That night he pulled out his diary and read the dream about the dark girl. He was convinced that his dream had become his reality, for even though he slept in an abandoned trailer on a hard metal cot, he slept in comfort, knowing that at last he had found The Way, and that he had followed it completely with all his heart.

The next day the boy began his duties as the factory bookkeeper. He stopped going to the tavern, for he didn't want to talk to the Mechanic when he was drunk. He bought himself a new suit since he felt he was starting an important chapter in his life. He remembered the three men who drove up in their brown cars on that first day, and wanted to make sure his appearance reflected the transformation he was feeling inside.

As the boy learned more from the financial records he also earned more respect from the workers. He became their champion and their leader, and the Manager was pleased. The boy spent his days listening to the customers and the workers, reading the financial statements and designing new techniques and products. He gained an ability to distill ideas, and the Manager agreed with most of them, and soon the boy was running the factory when the Manager was out visiting customers, who were placing more orders, even though the war continued and times were difficult across the country.

When spring arrived, the Manager called the boy up to his office a third time.

"Son, you have an incredible way about you," the Manager said, smiling. "You are able to see opportunity where others do not. You are able to come up with new ways of doing old things. And your ideas are welcomed by the customers. When you first arrived at my door, I thought you were just another gypsy boy on a journey to nowhere. But now I see you are an Entrepreneur who is on his way to be a great businessman."

"I am happy you think so," the boy replied in the most gracious way. "It is because of your kindness and coaching, for you have given me an opportunity to work here, and you took me in and gave me work and training and responsibility. So it saddens me to tell you that the time has come for me to return home."

"Yet another hadith comes from the lips of a Journeyman," the Manager sighed. He was disappointed, for he had come to love Musa as his own son. But he understood.

"When we first met, you said you were on your way to Baghdad, to become a great banker," the Manager replied.

"That was long ago, when I was misreading The Way," the boy explained, and he told the man his dream. The Manager lit a pipe and smiled as the boy described the dark girl and stacks of books and pages with numbers.

"Do not give up on your dream," the Manager said when the boy was finished, "do not rationalize it or change it to accommodate others. When I was young, my dream was to travel the world, to be an artist and live in the great cities of Europe and meet interesting people and have interesting conversations in cafes. But I never traveled."

"Why not?" the boy asked. He thought about the old worker oiling the bindery machines, and how he also gave up on his dream, and how sad and heartless he had grown to be.

"This factory was my father's factory, and my father's before him," the man said. "My destiny was handed to me; it was always to fill my father shoes. It is a good life, and my family is well off, but I am not always so jolly. Many times, especially at night, I wish I had not accepted my father's legend. But as I grew older, I realized that you cannot fulfill your dream and fill your purse at the same time."

"Why not?" the boy asked. "If you follow your dream, abundance will follow you."

"Perhaps, and it is true that now I have all the means to be that artist in my dreams. But I am overcome with fear, for what if, after all these years, I fail to be the artist I have always dreamed I would be? I much rather live in the dream than walk into it fully and see it not transpire."

The Manager let out a sad sigh, then suddenly smiled and pulled a small wooden box out from a desk drawer.

"I want you to have something for your journey. You are on The Way, following your dream, heading to a place I will never go. I want you to have this. It contains my grandfather's tools, the ones he first used to make books when he had his dream, in a hut where this factory now stands. They are not worth much, but they hold a special significance, so I hope you will care for them as I have."

The boy opened the box and inspected the large scissors, the carving knife, the stitching needle, the ruler and clamps.

"Thank you sir, but what do I do with these?" the boy asked.

"You are a creative one; when the time is right, you will know," the Manager said. "Often we receive an answer today for a question that is to come months from now. I wish you great luck on your journey, and should you return within the next year, I will ask you to stand beside me at this place, and I will double your wage again."

The boy could not believe his ears.

"Double?" he repeated.

"Yes," the Manager replied. "Because I believe you could run this business one day. My children have no interest in taking over the factory, for I have been a good father and raised them so that they could pursue their own dreams instead of mine. But I have put so much of myself into this factory that I cannot sell it to a stranger. But you, son, could take my place one day."

"I am honored," the boy replied, not knowing what else to say.

"Do not decide at this moment. Think about your dream, and how your destiny is with books. Look around...and consider that perhaps your treasure is here."

The Manager stood up and the boy knew the meeting was over.

That night the factory workers took the boy to the tavern for a celebration. They brought him wine, and the wine made him drunk, so he left abruptly and walked home and went to bed. When the dream returned, he noticed new things about the dark girl and the small room filled with books. He was still sitting in his room, writing in his diary, surrounded by mountains of books, and he looked up to see that the dark girl had entered, but as he turned towards her, he noticed something blinking outside the window. In the distance, he could see a massive skyline of tall black buildings against a gray sky, and the boy knew it was Baghdad, the grandest city in the world.

The boy woke, but he could still hear a voice far off in the night calling to him, a voice so sweet and intoxicating that the boy leapt out of bed and into the dark yard.

"I hear you, but I need to return home," the boy said as he stared up at the moon. He went back to bed but could not fall asleep, for he so wanted to hear the sweet voice call out to him again.

PART FOUR

The boy decided two things that morning: first, he would arrive early to the station and wait patiently for his bus, and second, he would not talk to anyone.

He walked through Samarra, and though the city was dark and quiet and haunting, the boy was not afraid, for he believed the universe would watch over him as he completed his journey. He was happy that he had left so early in the night, for even the sun had not risen and those who might cause him trouble were fast asleep. The bus station was closed and he sat against the doors for a long time until the dispatcher unlocked them. The boy bought his ticket and found a comfortable bench in front of the platforms, and though his bus would not leave for several hours, the boy sat patiently, for he did not want to repeat the trouble he had caused himself the last time he was trying to get somewhere.

Out of boredom he read passages from his diary, and though he knew many of them by heart, he enjoyed reading them again, especially the dream about the dark girl. He thought about how true the dream was and how it came to be, and he smiled.

"If you follow your dreams, you will be happy," he remembered his Mother saying, and he was eager to see her. He retrieved the dull white stone from his rucksack, the same stone he had pulled from the Professor's satchel when he was sitting on the rain-soaked gravel not far from where he now sat, beaten and bloody and penniless. The stone had helped him, and he thanked it quietly.

"I have one just like that," a voice said above him. The boy looked up. A man was standing next to his bench; he had deep black eyes and a black beard and wild black hair that fell about his face like a mane. The boy clutched his stone and turned away, for he did not want to talk to strangers.

"It's a dolomite, but you probably know that," the man volunteered. "It is beneath us, everywhere, all along the seaboard. Most of the gravel in these parts is made of either dolomite or limestone, plain old rocks usually, but you have a nice one there."

Still the boy did not acknowledge the man's presence.

"The ancients believed it brought about original thinking and relieved sorrow," the man continued. "In fact, the Algonquin Indians believed dolomite could help you remember that there is always a reason why things occur."

"Stones and Algonquians?" the boy thought. "What a strange coincidence to be talking about such things."

"I carry a stone with me, too," the bearded man continued. "I call it my gratitude rock. Every time I hold in my hand, or feel it in my pocket, I am reminded about how much there is in this world to be thankful for."

The boy did not say anything.

"Mind if I sit on your bench here, while I wait for my bus?" the man politely asked.

The boy nodded, and the man sat down.

"I thank you, and my gratitude rock thanks you. My name is Asad. I am a Scientist. Where are you headed?"

"Home," the boy finally spoke. He looked down, not wanting to engage in conversation, but then he noticed the ring on the man's hand.

"I went to the university, too," he added, slightly relieved.

"How delightful!" the Scientist exclaimed, shaking the boy's hand. "What a wonderful place, at least it was when I attended, which was long before your time. I wonder if the Old Professor still haunts the grounds."

"You knew the Professor?" the boy asked.

"Knew him? Why, the Professor was my favorite teacher," the Scientist replied. "It was the Professor that helped me see The Way. He was a mentor to me, and he instructed me in the most important lesson of all."

"What is it?"

"You would laugh if I told you."

"I promise I will not."

"It came not from a book, but from a bag of rocks. A simple gift, but it has helped me through some of the most important decisions in my life."

The boy smiled, convinced that the bearded man was not going to rob him.

"He gave me one, too," the boy replied. He reached into his rucksack and pulled out the small red satchel. To the boy's delight, the Scientist opened his briefcase and produced an identical red purse, tied tight with a black cord.

"You are the only one I have ever met with such a thing," the Scientist said, "which means we are meeting for a reason. The Professor said there was no such thing as coincidence, that nothing happens by accident. There is purpose to everything in the universe."

"Then what is the purpose of our meeting?" the boy asked.

"That's what's so fun about the mystery. Let's try to see what this is all about. When is your bus leaving?"

"Not for a while."

"Good, we have some time. We know that the Professor and his stones have brought us together. What else do we know? You said you were going home. Tell me, where are you coming from?"

"I was working in a book factory outside of Samarra," the boy replied.

"Did you study book manufacturing at the university?"

"Heaven's no. I studied engineering. Once I planned to be the best engineer in the world, but then I decided to be a banker in Baghdad. But that did not happen."

"Tell me what happened," the Scientist asked, and the boy did. The Scientist asked many questions, for he wanted to know all the details, as scientists tend to do. He had a hypothesis that the stones had brought them together, so he collected data to test his theory, but none of the facts of the boy's journey fell into any explanation.

"There is nothing in your story that connects with me," the Scientist said after a while. "But the stones are never wrong, so we must continue our research. Tell me about why you wanted to go to Baghdad in the first place, since that is where I am heading."

"You are going to Baghdad?" the boy asked.

"That is where I live and work," the man replied.

The boy told the Scientist about his dream of the dark child pointing to the page in the book. The Scientist listened quietly, and when the boy was finished, he smiled.

"Here is my theory of why we are here together, right now, on this bench, at this station," the Scientist purred softly, looking off into the distance. "I am supposed to tell you something, something that you may not want to hear, but it needs to be spoken."

"What is it?" the boy asked.

"You cannot go home just yet," the Scientist said. "It is not The Way. Your way is to follow your dream, honestly and completely, without pretending. You must continue your journey and travel to Baghdad."

The boy rolled his eyes, for he knew he had fulfilled his dream, and that he had already discovered his source of wealth at the book factory, which was exactly what his dream had predicted.

"I have enough money to get home and buy a gift for my Mother. There is no work in Baghdad for me, nor any place to stay. I am perfectly happy going where I am going," the boy insisted. "Thank you for your conclusion, but it is quite impossible for me to go where you are going."

"With that kind of attitude I would agree with you!" the Scientist roared, throwing his head back so that his thick hair danced about his collar. "But what if you change your attitude from impossible to possible? Let's talk about how you could go to Baghdad, and pursue this dream of yours!"

"I'd rather not talk about me so much," the boy replied. "Why don't we talk about you? Why are you here in this station?"

The man stretched out and spread his fingers wide like claws and rested them on his knees.

"I am a quantum physicist, and I just finished a meeting with some of the greatest minds in the field of energy," the man explained. "Not just any energy, but quantum energy, the energy of thought waves. They don't teach it at the university, but the Professor knew all about, in fact, I fashion myself to be one of his disciples on the subject. You see, everything in the universe, everything we touch and see and feel is made of energy. I am working on a theory for a problem concerning this energy."

"What problem?" the boy asked.

"Energy is dictated, like everything else in the universe, by certain laws, truths that are unbending and unyielding. One of the laws of quantum physics is that you cannot have a universe with the mind entering into it, because the mind shapes what is measured. Since everything is made up of energy, the energy of observation disrupts the energy of that which you are observing, so it becomes impossible to measure energy without influencing that energy. It's like measuring the temperature of water with a hot thermometer; the heat from the thermometer changes the temperature of the water. So the problem is, how can we really know energy if we cannot ever measure it?"

The boy knew some things about physics and mechanics from his studies as an engineer, so the Scientist's words were not too strange to him.

"The first law of thermodynamics dictates that energy is neither created nor destroyed," the boy replied.

"Yes, but it is constantly being converted. Look at your hand," the Scientist instructed, "and tell me what you see."

The boy obeyed and reported what he saw: skin and fingernails and freckles and blood vessels and some scars from his work at the factory.

"Do you know what your hand is made up of?" the Scientist asked.

The boy said he did, and went through the list, including blood and bones and hair and flesh and muscles.

"Yes, of course that is correct," the Scientist replied, "but look deeper. If your hand was under an enormous microscope, you could look beyond the cells and molecules and atoms, and you would see only a vibrating, pulsating mass of energy. Molecules are made of atoms, and atoms are made of energy that is shaking and vibrating and always on the move. And since everything in the universe is made up of energy…your rocks, my briefcase, this station, the moon, you name it…then everything in the universe is shaking and vibrating and always on the move. Including your thoughts. That's right; your energy is on a journey, just as your physical body is on a journey. And your energy is flowing and vibrating along with all the energy around you, never being created or destroyed, but always converting."

"You should write a book about it," the boy said.

"I don't have the courage to write a book," the Scientist admitted, "but when I complete my research, I will present my report to investors. There is one woman in the city who would be a perfect candidate to fund my work."

"Who is that?"

"The greatest Entrepreneur of our time. She is quite something; she started with nothing, and now she is extremely influential in all her business dealings. She has a keen interest in this energy I am studying. If I can present to her, I am certain she will fund my research, so I can solve this great problem of energy awareness. But she is impossible to meet because she is busy and important. So you see, each one of us is on a journey, and I have just told you mine."

"Who is funding your research now, if this Entrepreneur is not?" the boy asked.

"Last year I received a grant from a large bank in the city," the Scientist began, and when he told the boy the name of the bank, the boy nearly fell from the bench, for it was the very bank that Tamir had written on a slip of paper at the university. When the boy mentioned it to the Scientist, the man roared with laughter, and congratulated himself and the boy, for together they were getting close to what the stones were asking of them.

The Scientist persisted and tried to convince the boy to tap deeper into his dream, but the boy had long given up the idea of seeing Baghdad. He had been gone for five years and he was determined to go home. The Scientist asked many questions, using his analytical reasoning to hunt for clues to solve the riddle of the stones and why they happened to find one another in a Samarra bus station.

"Tell me more about your dream, for your dream has given us the best hints so far, so maybe it will again," the Scientist asked. "You said you saw buildings outside of your window in this dream. Can you describe them?"

The boy did, in greater detail than ever before.

"You just described my neighborhood!" the man exclaimed. "That's the Al Mansoor! You can see it from the window of my laboratory."

The boy felt a pang of doubt inside. Minutes ago he was certain he was supposed to go home. He had accomplished what he set out to do, and he had pursued and experienced nearly every aspect of his dream. But now a chance meeting with a stranger had boiled up too many coincidences, so many that he was compelled to think hard about his decision. The Scientist sensed this, and offered his advice.

"Do you remember what the Professor told you to do with your bag of stones?" he asked, and the boy nodded. "Ask the stones, for you are at a crossroads. You must decide whether to go back home as you have planned, or to venture into that innermost cave and follow your dream to its end. What will it be – your plan or your dream? You are running out of time, for two buses are about to leave this station, and you can only be on one. Ask the stones."

The boy knew the Scientist was right, and so he clenched his eyes and thought hard about his decision, and reached into the bag, and pulled out a stone. It was jagged; blood red and black in color. The boy did not know what it was or what it signified.

"I don't recognize it," the boy said. "It looks like red quartz."

"It's a garnet, and I know what it means. It is called the 'stone of commitment;' it helps you to take action." The Scientist reached into his pocket. "Remember I told you about my gratitude rock, that I keep with me at all times?"

The Scientist extended his hand, and the boy saw that he was holding a red garnet of exactly the same shape and size as the one in the boy's hand.

"Now what are the chances of that?" the Scientist laughed, and they both realized what the two garnets signified, so they conspired to plot how the boy might continue on his journey.

"You can trade your fare for one that will get you to Baghdad," the Scientist said after examining the boy's bus ticket. "As for room and board, the dormitories at the institute where I conduct my research are empty until the classes start again. I can arrange for you to live there until the end of summer, and if you assist me in my research, I will pay you a small salary, so you can buy food and such."

"That is too kind of you," the boy replied.

"But what is most important of all is that you continue on your journey. If the summer ends and you still have not found your treasure, only then should you consider going home, after you have searched with your whole heart."

The boy agreed.

"I have been gone for five years," the boy said. "What is five more weeks?"

The ride south was long and the bus made many stops, picking up and dropping off passengers, and waiting at times for the road to be secured.

"I have told you my journey," the boy said to the Scientist at one of the stops. "You must tell me more about yours."

The Scientist looked out the window, remembering when he was the boy's age. "Even before I met the Professor," he replied, "I knew I wanted to work in science. When the Professor told me about quantum energy, I was entranced. I felt like I had been told the most wonderful secret, so I embarked on a quest to learn everything about the energy that surrounds us and binds us. But the more I learned, the more I realized I could not understand it completely.

"One day, a wise woman told me about something she called karma. Some call it The Way, or destiny, or being followed by a guardian angel. I call it an energy force that connects and binds us all."

"What is this energy?" the boy asked.

"The energy I study is simple and complex all at once. Energy always is, it always has been, and it forever will be. Energy moves in and out and through form, and energy permeates everything and connects everything in the universe." The Scientist explained the logical, physical laws which defined energy, and though the boy listened intently, he became lost.

"I studied as an engineer, then worked in a factory making books," the boy said. "It is all because I followed a dream. That same dream brought me here on a bus with you."

"You are beginning to understand the energy," the Scientist said. "There is a law about attraction that says like energy attracts like energy. If you believe in yourself and pursue a path, then that energy is released out into the universe, and the universe will align to help you achieve your thoughts. The secret is that if you think it, it happens."

"I believe in my dream," the boy replied, and he shared more details about the dark girl and the room and the books, more than he ever shared with anyone, including his Mother.

When the boy was finished, the Scientist said, "I am not an expert in dreams; you can go to the East Side and the tarot readers will gladly take your money and interpret it for you. But I would say that since your dream takes place in your bedroom, it is about something that is very private and intimate. Are you involved with anyone?"

"No," the boy said, feeling sorry that he wasn't.

"Perhaps you will meet someone very soon," the man replied. "Now, there's this business about a window; perhaps it is a window to your soul, signifying hope and possibility in the future. Since you are looking out the window, your dream is about your awareness and your outlook on life, taking you outside, to Baghdad. The city is your community. Buildings also represent your own awareness, and since you mentioned they are getting taller over time, it means your own awareness is growing."

"And what about the dark girl?"

"I believe the child represents innocence, or perhaps your innermost feelings and repressed desires, but I could be wrong about that."

"And what about the book the girl handed to me?"

The Scientist thought for a long while. "A book could signify a slow and steady pace, or it was a premonition to your work at the factory. Since books represent knowledge and wisdom, that is a good thing to dream about. What does the book look like?"

"The cover is blue, with jewels attached to a gold edging."

"Blue is the color of wisdom and clarity, and gold is a spiritual signal. The jewels signify wealth, both physical and spiritual. This is a very important book the dark child is holding."

"But I cannot read the page," the boy replied.

"Except you see some numbers, a ten and a thirteen," the Scientist said. He ran a quick calculation in his head. "Those are good numbers to dream about. In numerology, that equates to a five, which is said to bring visionary ideas and action. Five means freedom and travel, if you believe in the meaning and influence of numbers."

"There are also words I cannot read."

"You will, in time," the Scientist answered. "Everything in your dream is connected, and if you are meant to read the page, then you will. Trust your dreams; trust the energy of the universe."

"Is that what quantum energy and metaphysics are all about, the power of belief?" the boy asked.

"One of the things," the Scientist answered as he gazed out the bus window. "But we will have plenty of time to talk about the science of thought and energy when we get to the laboratory. Right now, I want you to look there, and let your mind's energy embrace that."

The boy felt his heart leap into his throat as the skyline of the great city of Baghdad rose up from the horizon, basked in an emerald glow beneath the gray sky.

Musa simply uttered: "'and."

Paradise.

The boy focused all of his thoughts and love on what he saw, and he heard a voice in the city calling out to him, and he felt a happiness deep inside that he had never felt before.

☼

The boy lived in the dormitory and worked in the laboratory as the Scientist had promised. The boy was worried about finding his treasure, but the Scientist was even more worried about obtaining the funding he needed to continue his work. So the boy spent much of his time reassuring him that he had the power, the courage and the strength to obtain his goals, if he would simply heed what his own research told him was so.

"It is silly, that I believe in what I am researching, but do not believe in myself," the Scientist growled one day. "The energy of the universe is a powerful force, yet I am cowardly, because I am so analytical and seek hard evidence. But I cannot prove the existence of thought energy, just as I cannot prove the existence of love, or God. It just is."

"Then focus on what is, and what you need to do to accomplish what you have set out to do," the boy suggested. "Let's find a goal, an achievable one, which you can work towards, such as meeting the Entrepreneur."

"I only have one chance with the woman," the Scientist sighed. "I should send my proposal to other investors, to practice my presentation and refine my approach." He handed the boy a copy of his proposal. "You can be the first to review it."

"I will read it and make whatever suggestions I can," the boy replied.

The next day the boy delivered his comments. He found the proposal to be strong and compelling, but one thing bothered him.

"It reads well," the boy said, "but the appearance is lacking. Some wise men once said that how something looks on the outside reflects how it is on the inside. As it goes for factory yards and books and people it should go for funding proposals. You have a common cover, but this is an uncommon report which demands a cover that conveys your message."

"Excellent point,' the Scientist replied. "I shall go to the store and purchase a cover suitable for my work."

"That would not be good enough," the boy replied. "Your proposal is about the power of energy, about converting thoughts into things, about intention and gravitation and inspiration. You are proposing to demonstrate the power of The Way. Such a research proposal needs to be wrapped in that energy, with a cover that is infused with passion and purpose, like the one I made for my diary." The boy pulled his diary out of his rucksack. The torn and dirty cloth cover had been replaced with leather and wood, with fine stitching and carved relief on the front and back and spine.

"That is a beautiful book," the Scientist said, "it must be expensive to purchase such a thing."

"I made this myself," the boy replied, grinning and proud.

"How?"

"With tools that the Manager gave me, when I left the factory. The leather and wood is not expensive at all, but I took great care in constructing the cover and binding. As you can see, my energy radiates from it, just as your energy radiates from your proposal."

"You are right about appearances," the Scientist replied. "Your work is beautiful, and I would be honored if my proposal was combined with your craft."

A few days later the boy returned with a cover made of leather and cherry wood with a hand-stitched binding that included the Scientist's name carved in fine relief.

"It is remarkable!" the Scientist exclaimed. "I wish I could have one for every proposal I send out."

"I can make as many as you need," the boy said.

"You should not burden yourself tending to my needs," the Scientist replied. "While it is good of you to help me, be careful about making my journey your quest. Everyone has their own energy, and you should focus your energy on what you want, not what others want."

"I have considered that, and right now I want to spend my energy helping you, as you have helped me," the boy said.

"You are much wiser than you know," the Scientist replied.

The Scientist sent out many proposals to many investors, in hopes that someone would agree to meet with him, and so the boy spent his days and nights building leather and wood covers to fulfill the demand. As he searched for the materials he needed, he was drawn to a poor neighborhood on the opposite end of the city, near the river, and into a tiny shop hidden among the tall buildings.

The store was open but deserted, and the boy could tell that business was not well, for many of the items were old and covered in dust, which was the boy's good fortune, for the older woods and leathers were of better quality than the new ones sold in larger stores. He gathered the materials he needed, including tanned hides for covers, long thick leather lace for stitching, mahogany strips for binding and staining oil. When he was finished he approached the counter and rang a tiny silver bell sitting on the glass. In time a girl dressed in a green-and-white-striped smock appeared from the back room. She said nothing and began to make note of the materials the boy had laid on the counter, but she gazed at him with deep emerald eyes. The boy stared back, and it was as if all the energy of the universe rushed into the shop to greet him.

"Hello," the boy said.

She said nothing, but her eyes looked up again at the boy, and her lips formed a word that she did not speak. Their eyes reflected one another's for a long time, and the boy realized that she was speaking to him in a strange language. The boy wanted to say something but he could think of nothing, and his neck and back felt warm as he stared at the girl, unable to speak, unable to look away.

Then the girl smiled, and the boy smiled back, and it was as if the whole world smiled with them, and the boy felt the same feeling he always felt when he dreamed of the dark girl holding the book. Perhaps, the boy thought, he was feeling the energy that the Scientist spoke about, that he and the girl were vibrating in a similar frequency, but such technical terms could not describe the rush of confusion he was experiencing. He suddenly realized that every moment of his life had been spent thinking only about himself:

what he was, what he was doing, what he was to become, where he was going next. Now magically he was not thinking about himself at all; he was thinking about the girl. Who was she? What does she want? What will she become? Where is she going? His curiosity would not release him, and he could see that the girl was curious too, and they recognized one another's thoughts.

"I am frozen in time and space, feeling only the presence of this girl," the boy thought in wonder. "I do not know anything about her yet I feel strangely connected to her." Whatever secret language she was using, the boy could hear it, but could not speak it.

"Will that be all?" a voice boomed, waking the boy from his trance. A large woman in a drab gray dress stood in front of him, and the boy saw she was the merchant, for she held her hand out, indicating she expected money. The girl disappeared into the back room and the boy paid for his supplies and left.

The long walk back across the city seemed to take but a minute, for the boy walked on air the entire way, dreaming of the girl in the green-and-white-striped smock. He noticed things about the city he had never noticed before; the flowers that grew in the cracks in the sidewalks, the clouds that raced above the shadows of the buildings, the birds that rested at every corner and grassy park. Every color of the rainbow spilled down before him and painted the streets beneath his feet, and he never felt more alive in his entire life.

The next day he did not need any more materials, yet he set out across the city to the same shop, and when the girl appeared from the back room to make note of the materials he did not need, his eyes caught hers and he was able to speak, for he had rehearsed his words a thousand times the night before.

"Hello, again. What is your name?" the boy asked.

"Jena," the girl replied, and she did not look away.

"It is a beautiful name," the boy replied.

"It means 'paradise'," the girl replied, her eyes still wide.

"My Mother's name is Miriam," the boy replied, not knowing what else to say, for he had not rehearsed any further than this.

"Nobody buys anything here," the girl said. "What will you do with those things?"

"I am making book covers for an important document, for a Scientist at the institute, and they are going to all of the big banks across the city."

"It sounds very serious," the girl said.

"Oh, it is. It is a funding proposal for important research."

"What kind of research?" the girl asked.

"Research about the energy of the universe," the boy replied, trying hard to remember all the things the Scientist had told him. "It is a study about how we are all connected, and how everything has energy, and how positive energy and positive thoughts bring abundance, because of the laws of energy and attraction."

The girl smiled when the boy said the word 'attraction,' and he realized what he had said, and his face felt hot.

"I know a lot about such energy," the girl replied. "It can give you anything you want, if you embrace its power. But where I come from, we do not call it energy, we call it something else entirely."

Perhaps she is a religious girl, and she is referring to the story of the Bible or the Koran, the boy thought, but he was too embarrassed to ask, and the shop owner interrupted them as she had done before, so he paid for the materials and left.

The next week he returned to the store, having spent every day and night thinking about the girl. Again he approached the counter and rang the silver bell, and as before the girl appeared from the back room, but she was no longer wearing the smock.

"I was hoping you would need more supplies," the girl said.

"I do not need any more materials for my book covers," the boy replied. "I came back to see you. I want to tell you more about the energy in the universe and how everything is connected and the law of attraction. And I want to hear about what you call it and how you believe it works."

"I don't just believe it works, I know it works," the girl replied, "because I have been hoping you would come back, and here you are."

The boy felt his face turn warm again but he did not leave, and this time the shop owner did not interrupt them, for she could see her daughter smiling and happy, as she had once been.

Every day that summer the boy would rise at dawn and construct leather and wood covers for the Scientist, and every afternoon he would walk across the city to see the girl, and they would walk in the parks and feed the birds and talk until late into the evenings. He told her about his home and the old men and women in the hospital, and how he would care for them as if they were his flock. He told her about his days at the university and his trip to the green lake. He told her about his journey to Samarra and finally to Baghdad, to seek out a treasure he had still yet to find.

And he told the girl about his dream.

"A treasure does not have to be riches or gold or money," the girl replied. "You have a dream which you must follow wherever it leads you. For today, it has led you to find me, and now we are here together."

"I will find my treasure one day," the boy replied, "and when I do, I will share it with you."

"You already have," the girl said, "because the greatest treasure of all is love, and that is why I believe you have come to this vast city."

"What is love?" the boy asked, because though he knew what love was, he wanted to hear what the girl thought about it.

"Love is simple and complex, all at once," she explained. "Love always is, it always has been and forever will be. Love moves in and out and through form, and love permeates everything and connects everything in the universe."

"That sounds like energy," the boy said.

"Perhaps it is one and the same," the girl replied, and she kissed him, and the boy understood.

That summer in the city was the hottest recorded in history according to those that measured the weather, but the boy did not notice, for he had fallen in love. His thoughts for the girl made the days slip by like water through his hands. He took great pleasure in every moment, waking early in the mornings to make covers for the Scientist, and walking home late in the evenings from the girls' shop.

But the Scientist was fairing poorly. Every day he would deliver a new proposal to another investor, but each time his offer was rejected. When they called him back, they only asked where they could find the beautiful wood and leather cover he had included in his package, and the Scientist would refer them to the boy, who agreed to make more covers, for which he was handsomely paid. And so the boy made wooden and leather covers and sold them, and he would buy the girl flowers and wine. Soon he was working all morning and all afternoon and many evenings carving and binding his handcrafted covers. His walks with the girl became shorter, and he did not see her every day, but the girl understood his needs.

The boy's happiness grew as his money grew and his love for the girl grew. But as he became cheerful and alive, a great despair fell over the Scientist, for no investors had expressed interest in funding his research.

"I wish I had never met the Professor," the Scientist said one day, his head low and his skin hanging loose around his eyes.

"You cannot give up now," the boy replied. "You have planted a seed; your quest has germinated and though you cannot see it, the universe is conspiring to help you, just as it conspired to help me. Your wish is growing beneath the surface, and it will sprout any day, because if you wish it, it will come true. That is the law of energy that you taught me yourself."

"At least you are able to make money constructing book covers," the Scientist said. "But I am afraid my funding is all gone, and no investor has come forth to support my work."

"Then it is time to go see the Entrepreneur," the boy insisted.

The Scientist sighed sadly. "Boy, you are truly insane. It would be a waste of time, for the Entrepreneur is a very powerful woman who works in the tallest building in the city. She has amassed great wealth through her work and ideas and has no time for my small project. If these others will not support me, why in the world would she?"

"Because we will focus all of our energy to make it happen, like your research says," the boy replied. "Tell me everything you know about her, so we can devise a strategy."

And so the Scientist told him.

"We will succeed," the boy concluded, "for I have also been called an Entrepreneur. Your work has touched me, and so it will touch this woman who works high up above the city."

"You are more a jack of trades than an Entrepreneur," the Scientist said. "An Entrepreneur has a vision and focuses all of his resources and efforts to achieve that vision."

"I have a dream and I am following it," the boy replied, "and that is no different. It is time you contact her, so that she may see your work and decide for herself whether you are worthy."

"But I am afraid," the man replied.

"Fear of rejection is worse than the rejection itself," the boy replied.

The Scientist thought about what the boy said and realized he was right.

"Then I will try," he said at last with conviction, "with your help."

They did not have much time, for the Scientist had spent all of his funding and the students were returning to the institute, so the boy was told to make his leave of the dormitory. He stopped seeing the girl so he could help the Scientist improve his proposal, and he stopped selling book covers to the investors so he could craft a magnificent cover for the Entrepreneur.

The boy worked hard to help the Scientist, but sadness swept over him because the summer was over and he had still not found his riches. He prepared himself to return home, as he had promised himself he would do. He did not want to leave the girl, whom he considered the greatest treasure of all, but he did not have enough money to support her, and the merchant would not allow her daughter to marry a poor man. The boy realized it was time to go home and take up a skill, to learn his Father's trade and become a

Journeyman, so that one day he might return to the city and marry the girl.

He tried hard to hide his sorrow, but the Scientist could see it in the boy's eyes.

"I will promise that if the Entrepreneur funds my project," the Scientist said on his last day, "that I will hire you and help you find a place to live here, so that you may be close to the merchant's daughter."

"That would make me very happy," the boy said, and he threw himself into his work and constructed the most beautiful book cover he had ever made. When it was finished he gave it to the Scientist and said, "Take this, for this is my blood and sweat and tears, and send it to the Entrepreneur in remembrance of me," and he walked across the city to see the girl for the last time.

The girl was waiting and smiled as she always did when she saw the boy.

"I have been sitting in this shop for a long time, thinking about your dream and pondering your omens, and I am happy for you," the girl said. "But I am even happier for myself, for though you are still searching for your treasure, I have already found mine, and it is you."

The boy could not speak, and his eyes welled in tears.

"I know you must return home," the girl said, "but I am not afraid of losing you. You came to me because of a dream, and you found me because you were following The Way, which means our meeting was meant to be. And since The Way is for us to be together, then we cannot be separated by distance or time, for love transcends such things, as energy does.

"One day you will discover your treasure, and I will wait for you here in this shop, for you to return. I hope you will carry my love with you, wherever your journey takes you, so that we will never be apart."

"I promise that I will return," the boy replied, "and I promise I will have enough money so that I can take you with me, so we may journey together."

"Your love is the only promise I need," she replied, and they held one another for a long, long time.

As the moon rose over the city the boy walked home and his eyes welled with tears, one eye filled with tears of joy and the other with sadness, for he knew he carried her in his heart, and her love gave him strength and courage, and at last he understood what love was.

The next day the boy packed his belongings into his rucksack. He dressed in his nice suit, for he wanted to look his best when he arrived at home and embraced his Mother.

"It is a long bus ride," the Scientist said, "are you sure you want to ride the entire way dressed so formally? The police may question you."

"It is my journey, and I want to end it in full regalia," the boy smiled, and the Scientist smiled, and they embraced.

"This is a time for both of us to draw stones," the Scientist said, and the boy agreed.

The Scientist fetched his satchel and closed his eyes for a long time, then pulled out a small rock.

"Citrine!" he exclaimed, his black eyes wide like a lion's, for he recognized the stone to be an omen of strong self-esteem. "This stone suggests that abundance is coming my way, if I trust myself and act responsibly. This is a good sign for us both, for this crystal was thought by the ancients to bring great wealth."

The boy wished that he too would draw a citrine, but when he pulled his hand from his satchel, he was holding a small green stone.

"An emerald," the boy said.

"That represents beauty, for the goddess Venus," the Scientist added. "It is the holy color of Islam and an important color in the Arab League as well as in the Catholic Church, since it is the most natural and elemental color."

"That is not what I see," the boy said. "All I see is her deep green eyes staring at me on the first day we met, in her tiny shop. I hear her laughter and I smell her sweet breath and I feel her love and her warmth."

The Scientist smiled. "The emerald is a very special stone. It has the power to bring about love and promote harmony and bliss between two souls."

"She is with me always," the boy said. "I have found my love here in Baghdad. I asked for my treasure and the universe has answered. Now I must channel all of my energy and thoughts to accept this gift."

The boy clenched the stone in his hand and headed outside. He looked up into the sun and was blinded, but just for a moment, then he made his way north and walked across the great city for the last time, to board the bus that would at long last carry him home.

✿

On the other side of the great city, past the streets of the wretched fajarah and the zâlimûn, a woman lie in her bed, looking out across her room to where her jilbaab hung, her long, flowing garment that she wore when she wished to cover her entire body, head, face, hands and all. She had worn her jilbaab for many years, for now it was permissible for her to walk the streets and conduct her business in her own way.

Yet in the early morning, she longed for the days of the jilbaab. How it cloaked her true aspirations, how it hid her deepest dreams from her thoughts.

How her dunya, her life, had changed since she hung her garments on that wall, since she embraced the ghosts that whispered in her ears at night. Since she had become an Entrepreneur in the city of her birth.

This morning she felt out of sorts, more so than she had ever experienced. She wanted to stay in bed. Her calendar was not full and she was looking forward to tending to her own needs. But something compelled her to go to her office this day, so she dressed, not inher jilbaab, but in her business clothes, and thus she started her day as she had started every day for the past four years.

After her morning fara'id, the woman went up to the very top of the highest building in the city. It was a day like any other day, and it started the same way as it had for her for many, many years.

And yet she felt strangely different.

Her business was doing very well, but it had grown and matured, and thus had changed so much that it was foreign to her, and the work no longer touched her in the way it used to, when she first started. As she made more money and became more successful, she needed others to manage the daily affairs, and soon there were many people running her business and moving her from place to place and organizing her days, so much so that she no longer felt connected to anyone or anything, and this made her sad. It was the way of organizations, she realized, the mechanics of coordination and control of processes and people, and she was schooled by business experts and academics that she was following the correct rules of order and management. But still the world did not feel exactly right to her.

She began her work by reviewing the incoming messages of the prior day. The Mailman who managed her communiqués approached, holding a large package, but he did not hand it to the Entrepreneur.

"You don't need to see this one. It is from the institute," the Mailman reported. "Another request for money, for a project that has no relevance to our business."

"Let me see it nonetheless," the woman demanded. She caressed the intricate cover and held it to her nose, inhaling the sweet smell of leather and cherry wood. She inspected it front and back, admiring the tiny birds that were carved in the spine, and she found the place inside where the boy had inscribed his name. The beauty of the cover compelled her to read the proposal from beginning to end, and the Mailman waited until she was finished.

"I have not seen a thing of such beauty in this office for many, many years," the Entrepreneur remarked. "There is craftsmanship in this cover, and there is passion in the Scientist's proposal."

"It is about the energy of the universe and metaphysical nonsense, topics that have no practical application here," the Mailman explained.

"You should not judge that which you do not understand," the woman replied, and made a note to move the man to other duties, for she did not enjoy being surrounded by negative energy. "I want to meet this Scientist. Bring him in immediately, and find out where he purchased the cover for his proposal."

PART FIVE

His new suit did little to lift his mood, and the walk through Baghdad was the saddest walk of the boy's life. He tried to keep his spirits high but could not, and he bowed his head in shame in the shadows of the towering buildings. He tried to whistle, but his throat was dry and he wished for wine. His despair finally overwhelmed him and he stood at the corner of the street and watched the busy people pass by.

"Why have you forgotten me, universe?" the boy asked out loud, but the city was noisy and no answer or omen greeted him. He asked again, his voice louder, and the people on the street noticed him but paid no attention.

"Why won't you answer my Da'wah?"

"Back home to my Father, to work for him," he said, his eyes wet with sadness. "He was right; now I understand the Circle of Fatherhood. And I was right too, to follow my dream, for I have seen the room with the books and I have seen the great city. I did not find great wealth and I did not meet the dark girl, but I have discovered my love. I have found my soul mate and I have discovered my treasure. And even though my dream has forsaken me, and even though I must head home and my hands must become as my Father's hands, in my heart I know I will return one day for her, for love is the only journey worth taking."

He pulled his rucksack tight over his shoulder, feeling the weight of his stones and his tools and his diary, and he crossed the street towards the station.

"It is finished," the boy muttered.

Suddenly he heard his name through the bustle of the crowd and street traffic. The Scientist was running down the street after him, his arms filled with papers.

"The Entrepreneur has asked us in! She wants to see us both!" the Scientist panted, and the boy had to hear it again before he believed it.

"When?" the boy asked.

"Immediately! You must come with me! She asked for you, the maker of the cover. You must come, for I cannot see her without you!"

"My bus is leaving shortly," the boy replied.

"We are a team, and we must see her together!" the man explained, catching his breath.

"Why don't you ever want me to catch a bus home?" the boy laughed, and he wrapped his arm around the Scientist's shoulder, and they laughed together.

"You can catch the evening bus if you must," the Scientist replied. "You have waited five years and five weeks to go home; can't you wait another five hours?"

The boy considered this. "It would be a shame to quit now, I suppose," the boy said, "since your seed is just beginning to sprout."

The boy carried the papers and they walked north to the tallest building in the city, the same building the boy had seen in the window of his dream. They passed through a pair of enormous gilded gates and entered the grand lobby where a large painting was displayed. The boy looked up in awe; the painting stood three stories high and consisted only of the Entrepreneur's head. The size of her face was frightening and the scale so large that the boy was smaller than a single white tooth.

"That's her," the Scientist said when they entered the building, "that is the Entrepreneur. But she is much larger in person."

They were directed to a stairway, where several men questioned them and examined the boy's rucksack and the Scientist's papers. Then they were taken to the topmost floor of the building, high above the clouds, and told to wait.

"She will want to talk about how you made the report cover," the Scientist said. "Do you have any of them with you?"

The boy opened his rucksack and pulled out his diary. "Just this one. You may borrow it. Perhaps it will bring good luck."

"We should draw stones, but I am too nervous," the Scientist replied.

"It is not the right time, for you are on the right path, and you are about to step through the next door on your journey," the boy said, and the man agreed.

Many hours passed, but the Scientist and the boy did not talk, for the Scientist was quietly rehearsing his presentation and the boy was thinking about the girl. At last several men appeared from behind a door, and the Scientist was led into a large room, and the boy waited in the hall. The boy believed this was a good sign because he had heard that the Entrepreneur was very busy. If a woman of such wealth and importance would spend time with the Scientist, the boy thought, then she must be interested in his work.

The sky was turning gray when the Scientist finally emerged from the big room.

"What did the Entrepreneur say?" the boy asked.

"She asked a lot of questions," he replied, "but most of them were about you."

"I don't understand," the boy said.

"Neither do I, but the good news is she is interested in my work. Of course I need to address some things first. The bad news is that I cannot hire you until she agrees to fund my research, which won't be for many months. I am sorry."

"Do not be sorry, for you did everything you could," the boy replied, "and you will do more, if you do not give up."

"If it were not for you I would not have made it this far," the Scientist said as he hugged the boy. "You gave me nerve; the courage to keep going. I cannot thank you enough for that."

"It was always inside of you, the entire time," the boy replied.

The Scientist said goodbye and was escorted downstairs, and the boy was led into the large room, where the Entrepreneur sat behind a large white desk. She seemed much smaller than he had imagined.

"Tell me about yourself, young man," the woman demanded without introduction. She was a beautiful dark woman with jet black hair and a disarming white smile, but her expression was all business.

"That is a beautiful dress," the boy said.

"Thank you," the woman replied. "I am fond of the color purple. The Scientist didn't mention that you were well-mannered. That's good. Now tell me about your journey."

The boy described his home and his Father the plumber who was a hard man who worked hard and his Mother who was kind woman who loved everyone. He spoke about his decision to go to the university, and how a dream took him south, and how he was robbed and lost everything, but found work in a book bindery and later a research laboratory.

"And what did you learn from your journey?" the woman asked.

"That my treasure wasn't money, but a girl in a green-and-white-striped smock who works in a shop in this city," he replied.

The woman did not say anything. She spun her chair around behind the desk and stared out the window at the skyline below.

"They call me the Entrepreneur, the greatest of our time," she sighed, "but that is such nonsense."

"The Scientist says you are powerful and influential," the boy replied.

"Perhaps, in some circles," the woman sighed. "But not in the ones that really matter."

"I would like to be an Entrepreneur one day, like you," the boy said.

"You already are," the woman replied. "If you are in your heart, you are everywhere else. You and I are not so different. My mother died when I was young, and I went to live with my grandparents when I was only six. Back then folks called me 'Run-away.' Some in my family were not very nice, some even molested me, and so I ran away a lot. I moved in with my Father, who like your Father was a very hard man. I know he loved me, but he was very strict. So I fought against him. I fought and fought, I did bad things and I ran away and nearly lost my life."

"That is an incredible story," the boy said.

"The reason I tell you this is because it doesn't matter who you are or where you come from, or what happened in your past. You can be an Entrepreneur and become what I have become. All you need to triumph is what's inside of you."

"I believe that, sometimes."

"You need to believe it at all times, especially when you fail along The Way."

"The Way?" the boy repeated, recalling the Professor's words.

"It is called many things. Destiny, fate, the natural order, the energy of the universe, God, Buddha, Allah, Karma, Mother Nature…The Way has many names. It does not matter what it is called. It only matters that it exists, and that you believe in it."

"For me The Way came in the form of a dream. But I was afraid to follow the dream for a very long time."

"The thing that you fear has no power. It is your fear that has the most power."

"I have had luck, too. I met wonderful people along The Way, like the Professor and the Manager and the Scientist, and they helped when I stumbled and fell."

The Entrepreneur smiled. "Luck is simply preparation meeting opportunity."

"I know the Scientist will be successful in his research, and I hope you will fund him," the boy said.

"That is interesting," the woman replied. "Everyone who comes to see me asks me to help them. Yet you ask me to help someone else. Why?"

"Because I fear that the Scientist will fall into a dark age, a great depression, if he cannot complete his work. It has been a long journey for him, and he is so close. He needs success much more than I."

"Don't you want success, too?" the woman asked.

"Certainly I do. But success only gives you an opportunity to focus on what is really important," the boy replied.

"And what is that?"

"Making a difference in the lives of others. Being able to touch somebody's life. That's what it is all about. That is The Way as I have found it to be."

"It sounds as though you are in love," the Entrepreneur replied, smiling. "If you do what you love, the rest follows."

"Will you invest in the Scientist?" the boy asked again.

The woman paced behind her large desk.

"His idea has the power of passion behind it. But can it transform people's lives? If he can show me that, I will invest all the money he needs, because the Scientist is on the right track. He realizes that the greatest discovery of all time is that a person can change their future merely by changing their attitude. I learned long ago that if you are thankful for what you have, you'll end up having more. It is a simple law, one they don't teach at the universities. The reverse is also true: if you concentrate on what you don't have, you will never, ever have enough."

"How do you choose what to be thankful for, if the universe will provide you with whatever you ask of it?" the boy asked.

"It is not easy to make choices among all the things available in the catalog of the universe. So you choose the best you can, and align your thoughts and words with the intention to require more of yourself. Life is about choices, in fact, the whole point of being alive is to evolve into the complete person you were intended to be."

The boy considered this carefully, but still he did not know what he wanted to be.

"There is a simple truth, and your journey is the living lesson," the Entrepreneur said.

"What is that lesson? That I followed my dream and failed?" the boy asked.

"Exactly the opposite. What we dwell on is who we become. Since you were a young boy, you have been dwelling on pursing a single dream. You knew very little about the dream, you only knew with your whole heart that you must go after it. Your journey has not been a chase, but a lesson in discovery, for you have been searching for the answer to the riddle that the dream presented you. By dwelling on the quest, you have become the quest."

"But that is The Way, is it not?" the boy asked. "It is all about pursuing your dreams, about putting your thoughts and mind and heart behind what you believe in."

"That is correct. But ask yourself this question: all this time, what have you been putting your effort behind?"

The Entrepreneur sat back down and the boy thought for along time.

"I have been in pursuit of a dream," he said. The words hung over his head in the large room, so large and heavy that the boy could feel them.

"Exactly. So now tell me about this dream."

And the boy did, and he was not embarrassed.

When he was finished, the Entrepreneur smiled.

"You have done what few have been able to do," she said. "And now you know the secret that can give you anything you choose."

"What is that?" the boy asked.

"You have followed your bliss, which is at the heart of being an Entrepreneur."

The woman stood up and led the boy to the door and smiled. "I have enjoyed meeting you, and thank you for including me on your journey," was all she said.

The boy was escorted out of the building and back to the street. As he walked through the city to the bus station, he was puzzled, for not once had the Entrepreneur asked him about buying a book cover.

There were only two other passengers and the boy on the bus as it ascended north through the night. The boy thought hard about his choice, and saw that there were really only two paths in the universe, only one of two assumptions he could make. The universe, he believed, was either a friendly place or it was a hostile place, but it could not be both; you have to decide on one path. After meeting the girl, the boy could not imagine living in a hostile universe.

Yet even in a friendly world there seemed to be so many unfriendly, unhappy people. He thought of his Father, who caused him to arrive at the university many days late because he would only drive when it was convenient. But because of his Father's selfishness, the boy ended up in engineering and working in the library, which caused him to meet the Professor and Tamir and the Banker and the Algonquin, and that set him on a path north. Then there was Charon, the man in the red jacket in Samarra who robbed him and beat him, but he too was a gift, for without him he would have never met the Manager or the Mechanic or worked in the book factory, and he never would have met the Scientist, and, most important of all, he would have never met the girl.

The boy could not blame the gatekeepers that held him back or the guardians that blocked The Way, for without them, he would not have completed his journey. He forgave them and thanked them all for helping him find his ultimate treasure, in a small shop in Baghdad, dressed in green.

☼

The boy had hoped for snow, but the night was clear, except for the Târiq, the night-comer. It was late, and many of the lights in the surrounding homes had already been extinguished as the people went to bed. But the boy could not sleep. He had been walking for a long time. As he approached the mosque at the top of the hill, he looked up at the moon and smiled.

"No decision this time," he shouted at the dark minaret.

The heavy red door swung open, as it had years before, and the wind whispered in the rafters as it always did. He had not been in the mosque for many years, but yet he remembered where the Priest's table was placed and where the light switch hid on the alabaster wall.

When he turned the switch, the lights did not come on.

It didn't matter, for though it was dark he could see well enough.

He sipped from the metal bowl and sat down on the worn carpet. He thought about what had changed since his last visit to the mosque, during a thick winter storm. He thought about the places he had seen and the people he had met, and he thought about the girl.

The boy heard soft footsteps behind him and he rose to his feet, startled.

"Good evening, son," the Priest said. "You have not been to visit for quite some time. What brings you here so late this evening?"

"Long ago, this is where my journey started," the boy said, happy to see the Priest.

"You speak as though your journey has ended. Tell me, what did you discover on this journey?"

The boy looked up at the Priest, puzzled, for he had been contemplating this very question for some time. He was happy about having seen many things. He had traveled south, to the big cities, and had found his treasure, the love of his life. And though he was still poor, he was filled with happiness and love, and he told the Priest so.

"Isn't that what a journey is all about?" the boy said when he was finished.

"You followed your dream," the Priest said. "I had a dream, when I was a boy as you were, and like you I followed it. I met many people along The Way who helped me understand parts of the dream. Tell me, what did you learn about yourself along The Way?"

"I learned how to trust my feelings," the boy said, "and how to believe in myself, and how to put my dreams into action. It is called being an Entrepreneur. An Entrepreneur is a person who organizes an idea and assumes a great amount of risk to pursue it."

"Then I suppose each one of us is an Entrepreneur," the Priest replied, "for anyone who has a dream and pursues it fits your definition. But in this house, you are but a Journeyman."

"A Journeyman?" the boy repeated.

"It is bold of us even to assume we can learn His craft. A Journeyman is someone who has served an apprenticeship in a trade and is qualified to work in another's employ."

"I don't understand," the boy said. "Who's employ?"

"His, of course," the Priest said, pointing up. "But there are others. It could under the employ of Siddhartha Gautama or Peter or Lao-tzu or Jesus or Abraham or Confucius or Brahms or Muhammad. You can choose. That is the universal beauty of the craft. The Journeyman can always choose."

"But I am not religious," the boy confessed.

"What does that mean, to be religious? You are here, in a place of worship. You could just as well be in a temple or a church or a shrine or under a tree or at your dinner table. Do not confuse the procedures and orders of religions with your quest for being connected with the energy of the universe."

"What does a Journeyman do?" the boy asked.

"You do what you are. It means you pursue the craft you choose to its highest potential. Few do, for there are too many obstacles, too many demands, and many other people who get in the way with their own needs. But like your Entrepreneur, a Journeyman marches forward, and a Journeyman knows when he arrives; he knows when he is qualified and ready to be employed."

"Am I ready?" the boy asked.

"Not just yet, my son," the Priest smiled, "for your dream is not yet fulfilled. Dreams are like that. In my dream, I am sitting in this mosque on a snowy night, in the shadows of the great dome, alone and in the dark, questioning my faith. I was wondering if I was the only boy who still believed, when suddenly another boy walks in from the snow, kneels down and prays. It was an omen, an answer to a prayer. Then one day that dream came true."

"What did you learn?" the boy asked.

The Priest bowed his head. "I realized that belief is not about trying to reach all people. It is about reaching one."

The boy thought about the Nurse, who long ago said a smile was a gift, and if you could touch just one person, you could touch all people.

"Why is God so complex?" the boy said.

"God is both simple and complex, all at once," the Priest explained. "God always is, God always has been and forever will be. God moves in and out and through form; God permeates everything and connects everything in the universe. And when you are on The Way, God will ensure that the road will rise up to meet you."

The boy understood at last, because he realized that the way the Scientist described energy and the way the girl described love and the way the Priest described God were all the same way.

"Now hurry home, son" the Priest said. "Someone is waiting for you."

Outside the cool sharqi breezes blew up from the south, and as the boy walked home the wind reminded him of the city streets, and he could hear the girl's voice whistling through the trees and over the hills, and he wanted to run into her arms.

"My home is with her," the boy said softly, and the wind kissed his cheeks.

When he approached his Mother's apartment the boy could see that something was not right. The lights were on, and the boy worried that he would be scolded and called by his formal name, for even though he had grown to be a man, his Mother still held certain powers over him. As the boy pushed open the door, his Mother rushed into his arms, her eyes wet with tears.

"I tried to tell her everything," his Mother said, "and keep her from leaving."

"Who?" the boy asked.

"Hello, again," the Entrepreneur said. She was sitting on the couch holding a saucer. "We were beginning to worry about you. Fortunately your Mother makes a fine cup of tea."

The boy was alarmed, but he kept control of himself.

"Why are you here?" he asked the dark woman. "Did you give the Scientist his funding?"

"No, not yet, but I will in time. I am here for three reasons; to return something, to give you something, and to ask something of you."

"What is it?"

"First, this belongs to you." The dark woman handed the boy a small book in a wood and leather cover, engraved with birds.

"My diary!" the boy exclaimed. He had given it to the Scientist but had forgotten all about it until he was on the bus home.

"This is the most extraordinary little book," the woman said, confessing. "Yes, I read it cover to cover; I read all about your dreams and journeys. It is what compelled me to come visit you at this late hour, to ask for your help."

"How can I possibly help you?" the boy asked. "You are the greatest Entrepreneur of our time, and I am just a Journeyman."

"Sit down here beside me and I will explain," the woman said, motioning to the boy, and he obeyed.

"When I was your age, I had a dream and I followed that dream with all my heart and soul. I discovered very early that I could talk to people in a different way than most, and as people shared their experiences with me, and I shared those experiences with others, I was able to touch many lives. Over time I built an empire trying to reach others through any means I could. One of the most important ways I found was through books, through stories of struggle and inspiration and love and conquest and hope. It became my profession, and as my business grew, more and more people read the books and found inspiration, and it was wonderful. But as the business grew it became a machine, run by numbers and objectives, and I lost the joy of it all, because I could no longer see the love or passion that started it all, as it was in the beginning.

"Every night I have been asking myself: How do I get back to that creative passion? How do I find the energy and love in my work again? How do I bring the love of the craft of books and their stories to people all over the world? The answers have escaped me, until now.

"When I received the Scientist's proposal I knew I had found the answer. I was drawn to the cover, the one that you created, for it shined bright with love and energy and passion. It was the reason I read the proposal, and the reason I called you both.

"But I had to be sure that an object of such beauty had been constructed not by a robot or a mechanical man, but by a transitional man with all his heart poured into it. When I met you, I was convinced. Then this was handed to me, right after you left."

The woman pulled an amber envelope from her bag and handed it to the boy.

"It was tucked inside your diary," the woman said.

"That is the certificate my Father gave me, when I started my journey," the boy said. "But it is not worth much."

"Oh, it is to me," the Entrepreneur replied. "That is a certificate for ten thousand and one hundred thirty shares of a company. The shares were not worth much five years ago, but today they are, and I am pleased that you have held them while so many others have not."

"My treasure was in my rucksack the entire time?" the boy thought to himself, and he smiled and shook his head.

"But your certificate is worth much more than the shares they represent," the Entrepreneur continued, "because that certificate is for shares in my company, the company that I built with my heart and soul. When I found that certificate in your book, it was an omen that I needed to take action."

"What action?" the boy asked. He looked over at his Mother, who was crying because she was so happy.

"The book covers you created are works of art, made from the love and the energy of the universe. They are a manifestation of a powerful creative force; a force that lives within craftsmanship and the labor of love. I want to share such a force with everyone in the world, so I need you to work for me. That is the second reason I am here, to offer you employment in my company, to build and share your craft with readers all over the world."

"I am honored, really I am," the boy said, his voice humble and polite. "But I am just a Journeyman with a box of old tools, and the world is a big place."

"You will have whatever you need to produce your covers. I will hire a team and purchase a factory for you, and you will manage it all, and for that I will pay you a significant wage, and give you ownership in my company."

The boy smiled.

"I know of a book bindery in Samarra that would be perfect."

The Entrepreneur gazed at the boy's Mother, then back at the boy.

"There is a catch," she said. "You will have to move to Baghdad, and work beside me. I can arrange for a nice apartment for both you and your mother atop the newest building in the city."

The boy looked to his Mother, who smiled and nodded, but she could not keep herself from crying again for she was so happy for her son, and the boy was happy too, for he knew that taking care of one's Mother is the most important duty of all.

"Now, there is a third reason I have come to see you," the Entrepreneur said, "the most important reason of all. I have a favor to ask."

"What is it? Your wish is my command," the boy replied.

"We all have dreams, every one of us. I have read your dream and know it well. Now I wish to tell you mine. When I was a child, always running away from the pain of the world, I had a dream that I could fly. Every night I would dream that I was flying away to magnificent cities and countries, and I would fly over houses and buildings and gaze upon other children sleeping. And in my dream I had a magical power."

"What was it?" the boy asked.

"Whenever I flew into a child's room, I could see what they were dreaming, and I had the magical power to make their dream come true. When I visited a boy who dreamed of helping people, he became a great doctor. When I visited a girl who dreamed of peace, she became the leader of a faraway country. When I visited twins who dreamed of the land and sea, they built great businesses in farming and fishing. It was a wonderful dream, and I would pray for it to come to me each night. As I grew older I wanted to make that dream come true. That is what has driven me to build my business, to reach out and touch so many lives with messages of hope and love."

"I am not sure what this has to do with me," the boy said politely.

"I am getting to that," the woman continued. "In my dream I would always visit a boy who lived in the country, but this boy was different, because unlike the others he was not sleeping or dreaming. He was always awake, writing in a small book. I could not see what he would become, and I knew not how to touch this boy in a way to make his dreams come true. So I grabbed one of his books and I opened to a page."

"What happened to the boy?"

"When I showed him the page in the book, he gazed out of the window, and suddenly stacks and stacks of books appeared all around the room, and I understood that this boy, dreaming while he was still awake, would one day change the lives of millions of people."

"How?" the boy asked.

"By writing about his dreams and his journeys. In time his stories became beloved and cherished by people all over the world."

The boy did not say a word, and he sat beside his Mother and the Entrepreneur in deep silence, as if the earth had stopped spinning to allow the boy to catch up to it.

"The third reason I am here is to ask your permission," the woman continued, "to share the story of your dream and your journey with the entire world, so that you may touch others the way you have touched me."

The boy felt a great wave of emotion wash over him, as if a giant curtain had been lifted in his thoughts and the world was exposed to him in a new light. He realized the dream was more than a journey to find his treasure in a far away city. The dream was that his book, his diary, was the treasure itself.

Suddenly he knew without any doubt that he had found The Way.

Without saying a word, the boy reached for his rucksack and retrieved a small red satchel, and smiling at both women, he closed his eyes and reached into the bag and pulled out a small stone that sparkled and glimmered in the light.

"Is that a diamond?" his Mother gasped.

"I need to go," the boy said. "Will you take me?"

"Where?" the dark woman asked.

"To Baghdad, to find Jena. This belongs to her."

GLOSSARY

Muslim and Islam Terms, Persons, Places, Things and Practices

Abrâr - pious and righteous

Adab - manners

Alhamdulilah - *All praise is due to Allah.* To be said when happy and at other times.

'and – paradise

Bâtil – falsehood

Bismillah - "In The Name of Allah", to be said by the Muslim before proceeding to do that which is halal (permissible)

Da'wah - literally means "call", and in this sense it refers to calling to the Truth through preaching and propagation

Dunya - This world or life, as opposed to the Hereafter

Fajarah - Wicked evil doers

Fajr - The obligatory (faard) salah (prayer) before sunrise

Fara'id - Obligatory duties

Ghaib - Unseen

Hadith - Literally means "something new"

Halal - Permissible, lawful

Hasan - Good or acceptable. Used to indicate authenticity of some reports

Hijrah - Means migration. The Hijrah refers to the Prophet's migration from Mecca to Madinah. This journey took place in the twelfth year of his mission (622 C.E.). This is the beginning of the Muslim calendar. The word hijrah means to leave a place to seek sanctuary or freedom from persecution or freedom of religion or any other purpose. Hijrah can also mean to leave a bad way of life for a good or more righteous way.

Ilâh - Deity, lord, god

Insha'Allah - *If Allah will, If Allah wills it, if it is Allah's will, Allah willing, in Allah's timing and choosing*

Jahiliyyah - Extreme ignorance (jahl) and disbelief.

Jihad - to strive in the path of Allah.

Jilbaab - A loose-fitting garment covering the entire body, so that the shape of the woman is not defined but hidden, including covering the head, face, and hands.

Jinn - A creation of Allah made from smokeless fire.

Ka'ba - A square stone building in *Al-Masjid-al-Haram* (the well-known mosque at Makka)

Kâfirûn - Disbelievers in Allah, in His Oneness, in His Angels, in His Books, in His Messengers, in the Day of Resurrection.

Khabîth – evil

Khalafee - A person who chooses to follow the later generations of Muslims as opposed to the early ones

Khutbah - A speech or sermon. It is sometimes used to refer to the sermon given during the Friday congregational prayer.

Laghw - Dirty, false, evil vain talk

Maulâ - Lord, Helper, Protector, Supporter, Patron

Minhaj - Methodology, e.g. methods, rules, system, procedures.

Munkar - Wrong, evil-doing, sins, polytheism, disbelief, etc.

Nafs - Adam or a person or a soul etc.

Qabîluhu - Satan's soldiers from the jinns or his tribe

Qiblah - Prayer Direction

Sadaqa - Deeds of charity done in Allah's cause

Salaf - Literally means "those (from history) who precede, have gone before".

Salâmu-'Alaikum - Peace be unto you. The greeting between Muslims.

Tâbi'een - Those who met the Companions of the Prophet

Tâghût - Anything worshipped other than Allah, i.e. all the false deities. It may be shaytaan, jinn, idols, stones, sun, stars, angels, human beings, etc.

Taqleed - To blindly follow a person whose following is not based on proof and does not rely upon knowledge.

Taqwa - acting in obedience to Allah, hoping for His Mercy

Târiq - Night-comer, the bright star

Tayyib - All that is good as regards things, deeds, beliefs, persons, foods, etc.

Walî - Protector, Guardian, Supporter, Helper, Friend etc.

Zâlimûn - Polytheists and wrong-doers and unjust.